GUARDIANS

Book 4: The Triplex

GUARDIANS

Book 4: The Triplex

NEW YORK TIMES BESTSELLING AUTHOR

Lola StVil

GUARDIANS: THE TRIPLEX

By Lola St.Vil

Copyright © 2012 Lola St.Vil

Formatting by Dallas Hodge, dalhodge56@gmail.com

Cover design by Renu Sharma

TABLE OF CONTENTS

This book is dedicated to Gaurav Sharma:
You are the definition of courage and strength.

And it's not fair that you are a brilliant artist
And I have trouble with stick figures.

You inspire me.

This book is also dedicated to
Anyone who dares to travel down roads not taken

Keep going…

BOOK 1: EMERSON BAXTER

"Out, out, brief candle! Life's but a walking shadow, a poor player,
That struts and frets his hour upon the stage,
And then is heard no more..."

—W. Shakespeare

CHAPTER ONE: ISIS & DEMETRI

"I'm dead!" I gasp as I slowly fall to the ground. He stands before me and proclaims victory.

"Yes! I win again!" he shouts with the most adorable evil laugh. I sneak a peek and he scolds me.

"You're dead, Green Goblin. You can't open your eyes," the five-year-old warns me.

"Okay, but if I'm dead, I'm taking all my candy with me." My neighbor, Ben, thinks long and hard over his dilemma.

"Okay, Emmy. You're not dead, but you have to give Spiderman all of your candy."

I get up from the floor and fake a mean look. He stares me down and sticks out his wrist as if to release his "web." It's hard to keep a straight face when confronted with the cutest Spiderman in Manhattan.

"Okay, okay. I give up."

"Yes!" he exclaims as he runs past me and heads over to the coffee table. He takes the bags of candy (the result of an exhaustive night of trick or treating) and dumps them out onto the table. Ben then begins to divide them. He gives me all the boring stuff (candy corn, raisins, trail mix) and takes the good stuff for himself.

Just as he is about to devour the candy, his mom enters.

"Hold it!" she warns.

He turns to look at her with wide, hopeful eyes.

"What?" he asks, knowing very well why his mom stopped him.

"One piece. The rest is for later."

"But, Mom—"

"I mean it. Now say good night to Emmy and thank her for taking you trick or treating."

"Thanks, Emmy," he says, giving me a hug.

I hug him back. And try hard not to pinch his cheeks. I know he hates that but he really has the most pinch-worthy cheeks I have ever seen.

"Rio is waiting out in the hallway for you, Em," Ben's mom informs me.

"Okay, thanks." As I am walking out the door, Ben's mom stops to look at me. She's looking for something to say to make it all better. It's been a month since my mom was murdered. She wants desperately to say something that will take away the grief. I get that look of sadness and helplessness a lot from people who knew my mom.

"Emmy…" she starts. I give her my most reassuring smile and tell her what a great time I had. Thankfully that is enough to satisfy her. I head out the door and find Rio patiently waiting. Ben runs out to the hallway and says hello to Rio. Before Rio even has a chance to reply, Ben launches into the events of the evening.

"There were a million Spidermen, but I was the best, right, Em?"

"Absolutely," I confirm.

"I'm sorry I missed it," Rio says, smiling.

"You can come with us next year. Emmy and me are going to dress up next year too, right?"

Rio and I exchange a look.

Next year…

I inhale deeply and address Ben.

"It's a date, Spiderman."

He beams and runs back into his apartment.

Once Ben's door is closed, I address Rio.

"I thought Marcus was picking me up."

"He was busy."

"I figured."

Rio studies me.

"Emmy?"

"Yeah?"

I know he's reading my Wave. I know there are a lot of colors. I'm certain he knows the truth that I have been hiding from everyone: I'm afraid to die.

"If you want to talk…" Rio begins.

"Let's just focus on Marcus. He is not dealing with this well."

"And you are?"

"No, but all I have to do is die. He's the one who has to take the life of someone he loves."

"I know you're concerned about Marcus, but his concern at the moment is you. Don't you think you should admit to him that you're terrified?"

"Will that change anything?"

"Maybe not, but you two need to talk about it."

"All we've done is talk. But no amount of talking will change the fact that a Dy cannot be cast out without killing the person it's in. It's never been done."

"I know but…"

"The Sage was right. The minute Marcus found out the Triplex was in my eyes and he didn't kill me to get it, Marcus betrayed his mission."

"So, what now?"

"Now we help him get back on track."

"You mean we help him kill you?"

"He's the only Guardian who can take a human life."

"Just because he can, doesn't mean he will."

"I could do it myself."

"You heard the Sage. If you die by your own hands, the map will go into limbo. We would have to start looking for it all over again. And since we are only allowed a year for this mission, there just isn't enough time."

I sigh and lean against the wall for support.

"Maybe there's a way to cast out—"

"Rio, let's not do this again. We have looked for ways to get around it; there is none. Marcus has to take my life. He has to do it before midnight of the New Year."

"So how do you think we will get Marcus to agree to kill you?"

"I think first we have to get him to stop looking for an answer."

"He'll never stop."

"Then we just have to get him to understand that there is no saving me."

"I have read Marcus's Wave, Em. He would rather die than give up on saving you. In fact, his drive is the only thing keeping him going. It's like he doesn't see the world anymore. He only sees you."

"We can't let the world end because of me."

"The decision isn't ours. It's all Marcus."

"Where is he?" I ask.

"Same place he's been for the past month…"

I walk into the Guardians' home and find him sitting exactly where I knew he would be—on the living room floor reading. Every inch of the room is covered with books. They range from the history of the council to angel fairytales.

He has read and reread every one of them. Every book says the same thing: a Dy can't be cast out without killing the being it was hidden in. No matter what, in order to get the Triplex, Marcus has to take my life. There is no question about it: my angel is in hell.

"Hey," I call out softly from the doorway.

He doesn't answer. I don't think he even knows I'm here. I walk up to him and tap him on the shoulder. Startled, he looks up at me. There's sadness in his eyes. But the sadness can't take away his inexplicable beauty. He's hot no matter what's going on.

It's just my luck, I fall for a gorgeous angel and what do you know? He has to kill me…

"What? What is it? What's wrong?" Marcus asks, on high alert. His biggest fear aside from having to take my life is that the Akons will find out about the Dy and come after me, or worse, Lucy will.

I'm actually okay with Lucy coming after me. I have wanted to kill her since she murdered my mom. I know I'm no match for her but I don't care. I would like to strike her just one time. I don't tell Marcus because the thought of me going up against the source of all evil doesn't sit well with him.

"I thought you were going to pick me up and we were going to the parade?"

"Yeah, on Halloween, right? That's days away."

"It's tonight."

"Oh. Sorry," he says, never taking his eyes away from the pages that lie before him.

"Marcus, you need to Recharge."

"I will in a minute."

"No, you need to rest now."

"What I need is a way to help you."

"Please go Recharge."

"Not yet."

"Marcus—"

"No!" he barks loudly. The other angels appear from various rooms of the house.

Marcus sighs heavily, runs his hand through his hair, and kicks a stack of books across the room. The force of his kick causes the books to embed into the wall.

"We're okay," I call out to the others. Miku, Ameana, and Jay all look to Rio to see if he agrees. Rio reads Marcus's Wave and signals that he has calmed down. Thankfully, they leave us alone. I sit down on the floor beside my boyfriend.

"Why don't we get some air?" I offer.

"No, I have to read this."

"Marcus, you've read that book already. You've read all of these already."

"Yeah, and I will read them again until I find a way to get the Triplex without…"

"What if there is no way?"

"There is a way. And I will find it."

"I just want you to stop torturing yourself."

"So what am I supposed to do?"

"You have to get the Triplex out of me before midnight of the New Year, that gives us only two months."

"Two months to do what?"

"Be with each other."

"So what, I just give up and take your life like it's nothing?"

"I'm just being realistic."

"I don't need you to be realistic. I need you to be supportive. I need my team but they all just left."

"They've been supportive. They have scoured the world trying to find some kind of way to get the Triplex without hurting me. For the past month all your team has done is support you. Support us."

"We can't stop now. I'm close to something. I know I am."

"The Sage—"

"Screw the Sage."

"Marcus."

"Emmy, all he wants to hear is that he was right: that I abandoned my mission because of you."

"It's his job to tell us what he knows."

"He doesn't know crap. He should have told us where the Triplex was. We could have been finding a way to save you since we got here. Instead, he let us go on some wild goose chase, knowing damn well the Triplex was in you."

"He didn't know. He just knew that our love would get in the way of the mission. And it has."

"I don't care about the mission."

"You do. I know you do. This isn't just a mission. It's about saving humans, and you have always tried to do that."

"Emmy, I can't lose you. I won't."

I look into his eyes and I see the human he used to be. The teenage boy that fought with everything he had to stop his mom from taking drugs; the boy who was unable to keep his family together.

"Okay, let's keep looking," I say, taking his hand in mine.

Relieved, he kisses me quickly and goes back to reading. It's funny that a kiss so quick can linger on my lips and make me weak. I don't know if it's because Marcus and I weren't able to kiss till a few weeks ago, but I crave his touch every time like it was the first time.

Chapter One: Isis & Demetri

As I flip through the book nearest me, I think back to a month ago when Marcus and I first told the team where the Triplex was. I have been to hell. That experience came very close.

After Marcus told them the news, the room went completely silent. It was the kind of silence that rings so loud, it could make your ears bleed.

"Someone say something," I said to them. Then I realized what stunned them wasn't the news but the actual sight of a micro-map inserted in my eyes. They all stood up and studied me. I understood the fascination. I looked at myself in the mirror for hours when I first found out. I still did, as if looking at it would make it go away.

Ameana was the first to speak.

"The Sage was right. You are betraying your mission."

"Really, Ameana? That is the first thing you can say?"

"Well, it's true. You know where the Triplex is but you won't get it. So, he was right. You have betrayed the mission."

"We don't know he's going to betray anything," Miku said.

"Pretty, we all know Marcus isn't going to kill the human," Ameana answered.

"This is jacked up…" Jay said, filled with frustration.

"So, what now, Marcus? You're going to let the whole world go to hell so you can save one girl?" Ameana asked.

"You can't put your hatred of Emmy aside for one second to try and figure a way to help?"

"I already put my feelings about Emmy aside. Why do you think the two of you can go up to the mountains and screw each other every night?!"

"What, we don't—we haven't—Ameana, what is your problem? How long are you going to keep hating me?"

"This isn't about you. It's not about Marcus. It's about the world. It's about saving billions of lives," she barked.

"Emmy, you know you my girl, but Ameana's right. We can't let Lucy destroy humanity," Jay said sincerely.

"I know," I assured him quietly.

"""

"We need to talk about options," Marcus begged.

"It's a Dy, Marcus. There are no options," Rio said pensively.

"Well, we thought you were dead and there were no options. But you're standing here now, aren't you?" Marcus snapped.

"This is different," Miku protested.

"How can you be so okay with killing her, Miku? Emmy has done everything to try and help you. Now you want her to die?" Marcus accused.

"She's not saying that, Marcus," I said, defending her.

"Whatever. We are not killing you," he assured me with absolute certainty.

"Let's talk to the Sage. He might be able to help," Miku offered.

That's when Marcus and I exchanged a quick glance.

"We already talked to him," I confessed.

"What did he say?" Miku asked, her red-tipped wings flapping against the air.

"He said I should use this time to say goodbye to family and friends," I replied softly.

The twins exchanged a look of deep concern and Jay lowered his head. The despair and anxiety made it hard to breathe. Marcus held my hand tightly.

"Look, guys, I'm not saying it will be easy, but we have three months. We might be able to find a way to get the Triplex out of her. I really believe that," Marcus said, softening his tone.

"Yeah, maybe it's possible," Jay said softly. I wasn't sure he really did believe but it helped to hear it. The twins consulted each other silently, then they signaled that they would help. We all turned to Ameana.

"I think this is a waste of time. You cannot cast out a Dy. It's a death sentence for the person it's inside of. But fine, I will help."

I could actually feel the relief flowing through Marcus's body.

Rio then quietly asked the question that Marcus had been torturing himself with.

"We're willing to help Emmy, but if all our efforts fail, are you willing to do what needs to be done?"

Chapter One: Isis & Demetri

So here we are in the living room a month later and we are no closer to finding a way to save me. I keep helping Marcus search because he needs me to do it. In truth, I'd rather be off somewhere else.

Marcus interrupts my thoughts by asking if I think there is any truth to the story of "Blue Rain." I tell him no, but he insists on repeating the Para fable for the millionth time. It's a story about Isis, a Para angel, and Demetri, a demon. The two of them fell in love. The council forbade them to unite, fearing it would throw off the balance of good and evil.

"One evening, Isis and Demetri fled their homes and met here on Earth. The council sent the Omari after them. They were sought-after fugitives. They ran to the ends of the earth but still the Omari tracked them down.

"That's when they learned a shocking secret. Isis had given birth to triplets, three girls who were half demon, half Para. The news of the three sisters traveled throughout the Angel world. Furious with the potential danger to the balance of the world, the council devised a plan. They made an Amulet containing unrivaled power and they told Demetri he could have the Amulet if he found the key.

"They then broke the key in three pieces. Each of the babies had a Dy cast on them containing a piece of the key. The only way for Demetri to open the Amulet and gain infinite power was to kill all three of his children.

"Weeks afterward, the council checked to see if Demetri had given into his natural instinct and destroyed the babies. But so far Demetri had not given in to temptation. The council grew weary and once again Isis and Demetri were being hunted down.

"One day Isis came home to find all three cribs empty. Demetri was gone. So was the Amulet. Isis, having lost her children and the love of her life, began to cry. Her heartbreak was so powerful, so pure in its sadness, she did something no angel had ever done before. She cried.

"It's said her grief was so strong, it pulled the blue out of the sky and poured itself into millions of raindrops. It rained a blue rain for forty days and forty nights. A group of Para angels, helmed by their then-leader, Noah, built the ark to help humans take shelter.

"When Atourum learned that Demetri now had power, she sent demons to destroy him in fear he would someday overtake her.

"It's said that in the end, Isis cried herself to death. And when it's a bright sunny day but a sudden burst of rain appears, it's the heaven's dedication to Isis."

"That story gets sadder every time I hear it," I tell him.

"Now angels just use her story as an expression: yeah, I like so and so, but it's not blue rain."

"Oh, so…am I blue rain worthy?" I ask teasingly.

He used to pull me close and hold me when I would joke around like that. Now, he tells me to be serious and focus. I'm resigned to the new "all business" version of Marcus.

"I guess the council always hated couples, huh?" I ask.

"They're real serious about maintaining balance."

"But they tempted Demetri. If they hadn't, he would have still been with Isis."

"That's a point Para angels argue about in bars all over Daraquin."

"I didn't know the city of Paras had a bar."

"Yeah, the Coy keeps flowing."

"Have you ever been to one?"

"No, I always wanted to."

"So, let's go."

"Go where?"

"Daraquin."

"Emmy, be serious."

I am serious. I am going to lose my life in a few weeks and I just want to spend as much time as I can with you. Please, please stop trying to fight the inevitable…

I want so much to say my thoughts out loud, but I know it will only upset him. So once again, I play along.

"So what is it about this story that you think could help?"

"The Amulet. If it's still around, maybe it will give me enough power to somehow get the Dy out of you."

"It's just a story. It's not real."

"Noah's real. He was at the summit."

"It's a fable. Some parts are true and some aren't. I mean, blue rain? C'mon. How strong would your pain have to be to drain the blue from the sky?"

"I know, but sometimes there are clues in stories. In songs…"

"And even if it was, I'm sure Lucy would have destroyed the Amulet along with Demetri," I protest.

"I just thought…"

"What?"

"I don't know," he admits sadly.

"We have traveled to far-off villages looking for accent elixirs that would help and we found nothing. We sought out powerful Paras in Daraquin, we even went to an eye doctor," I plead.

He looks up at me, and even in Difi, he was in better spirits. I sit on his lap and look into his eyes. Even the thought of getting to kiss him causes my heart to leap. He leans in and presses his soft lips against mine. Blood rushes to my face. A familiar, delicious spark zooms down my spine. I kiss his bottom lip and go in hungrily for more.

Suddenly he breaks off the connection.

"What's wrong?"

"There's a book I read last week—where is it?" He practically throws me off of him and rummages around in the stack of books.

"Marcus, enough," I beg.

"Wait, there's just one more thing I need to look up—"

"Enough."

"No. I'm close to—"

"I SAID ENOUGH!" I take the book in his hand and hurl it across the room.

He looks at me, puzzled.

"I can't do this anymore."

"Emmy—"

"NO. I have sat here for weeks watching you tear the world apart looking for hope where there isn't any. You cannot save me. I am going to die."

"You aren't going to die."

"I know this is difficult. I know it hurts you. But it's my death and you're leaving me with no room to grieve. Every second of the day I have to think about putting up a brave face for you. I'm tired. I'm so tired."

"Emmy, I—"

"Stop holding on to hope, or clues or fables."

"Then what the hell else am I suppose to hold on to?"

"Me."

"You don't want me to hold you. You want me to say goodbye to you."

"You were going to have to leave me anyway."

"That is not the same thing," he protests.

"Why not?"

"When we go into the light, you're still supposed to be alive. You can still have a life after us. After me."

"After you? You think there's something 'after' us?"

"The point is we were supposed to come here, get the map, and let you go on with your life. You aren't supposed to die."

"Neither was Reese or Sara or my mother. But they did. They died and I will, too. Nothing you do is going to change that."

"Why are you so okay with dying? What is so wrong with your life?"

"I'm not okay with dying, but I am also not okay with spending the time I have left scouring old books."

"What if there is something here that can help you?"

"What if there isn't?"

"I won't accept that."

"You have to be realistic."

"You want me to tell you that I am okay with you dying; I'm okay with being the one who ends your life."

"Marcus, I'm begging you. Please, give me this one thing: accept the situation."

There's desperation so deep in my voice, it goes through my soul like ripples in a pond.

"Emmy, you could dive to the ocean floor and barely reach the depths of how much I love you. I would give you all my lifetimes, my wings, my soul. But please, don't ask me to accept this."

He pulls me close and whispers in my ear, words a First Guardian should never say:

"I'm not strong enough…"

CHAPTER TWO:
FIREWORKS

It is weeks later, and still, we are no closer to finding a way to save me. I wante to suggest we have a Thanksgiving meal together, but I didn't. Marcus was in no mood for a get-together. So the month of November passed in a blur of tension and false hope, just like the month before it.

We are now in the second week of December. I'm in my apartment getting ready for the final days of school. For most students it's the final days before winter break. For me, it's just the final days.

Almost everything in the apartment reminds me of my mom. That's why I spend most of my time at the Guardians' house. My uncle Max wanted me to come stay with him and his family but I said no. Not only would Marcus not let me out of his sight, I felt like leaving the apartment was somehow like leaving my mom. That's why no matter how long I stay away, I always come back home.

Uncle Max wasn't okay with me staying here alone. I had to get Jay to Convince him that I was fine. My uncle isn't the only one concerned. Ben's mom brings me food all the time. Unlike my mom, she's a great cook. But no matter how amazing the meals are, I tend to take only a few bites. Knowing you are going to die does something to your appetite.

I have not gone inside my mom's room since she died. I can't bring myself to open the door. I know it's crazy, but with the door closed, I can always pretend like she's behind it: she is somewhere in her bedroom rereading a Bronte novel and at any minute she's going to call me because she got to a really good part and wants to read it out loud to me. It's like with the door closed, she's still alive.

"Hey, we're going to be late for first period!" Miku shouts from behind the door. Marcus insists I go to school. He doesn't want me to get behind.

We all know that it's silly, but so is recording your dead mom's favorite show, like she's coming home to watch it later. I guess denial is the great new drug. And Marcus and I are addicted.

"Miku, come in," I shout back as I try in vain to do something with my hair other than a ponytail. I swear if I was given the choice of powers, it would be the power to make my hair look like it came out of a glam mag. The power to take out demons is cool, but maintaining perfect hair, that's real power.

Miku comes into my room and shakes her head at me.

"Your hair looks fine, it's time to go."

"I know, it's just…" I sigh and put it in the same old ponytail it's always been in.

"We need to go, don't make me get Redd on you," Miku jokes. It's great that she can laugh about having Turned, but deep down I know she's still dealing with a lot of guilt from having murdered someone. If she had forgiven herself all the way, the crimson would be gone from the tips of her wings.

Since Redd has gone back to being Miku, there are still some angels who fear her. Sometimes they see her and start to tremble. She goes out of her way to be nice to them but the fact is, once you rip some guy's heart out with your bare hands, it's hard to make nice.

"Pretty, can I ask you a question?"

"I knew it!" she shouts.

"What?" I ask.

"It was Rio's turn to come up here and get you, but he said he wanted me to go. I asked him why and he said 'no reason,' but I swear there was a little smirk in his voice. He read your Wave and he knew you wanted to ask a question that was embarrassing."

"Well…"

"I'm gonna kill him!" she says to herself.

"Okay, I don't have to ask," I say, giving her my best 'puppy dog' sad eyes.

"Okay, okay. What is it?"

I perk up and close the door behind her. Even though we are alone, I feel better knowing we're behind closed doors.

"How do I get Marcus to have sex with me?"

"You're a girl. He's a guy. Consider it done."

"Yeah, I know he *wants* to, but how do I actually *make* him do it?"

"Emmy, we're going to be late."

"Pretty, I am going to die in a matter of weeks. I don't want to leave this world without having made love to Marcus. Please help me; how do I seduce him?"

"Just do what you normally do with guys."

I avoid her eyes and try to play it cool. "Oh, okay. Sure. I didn't know if angels were different in some way."

"Marcus is your first boyfriend, isn't he?"

"Kind of…"

"You have to be confident when you approach him. Don't do the 'Emmy-self-doubt' thing."

"I don't have a—" She raises her eyebrows.

"Okay, I won't do that," I vow.

"Good. Next you look in his eyes, then slowly lean in like you're about to kiss him—"

"Wait! I need to take notes," I announce as I scour the room in search of pen and paper.

"Damn it!" I shout as my search turns up nothing. I turn my room upside down. Miku calmly takes me over to the bed and sits alongside me.

"You don't have to write it down. All you need to do is be in control. Be confident. And remember he wants you."

She suppresses a smile and lets me go over it yet again.

"Okay, if I am confident and all the other stuff you said, I should be able to seduce him."

"It's a good bet."

She smiles and I get my stuff to head out the door. Then a thought occurs to me. It stops me dead in my tracks.

"I don't have any seduction clothes!"

I run to my closet and begin to pull everything off the hangers. It is exactly as I fear. All my clothes are jeans, sweaters, and cartoon T-shirts.

"You aren't trying to sleep with him this morning, are you?"

"No, but I need to go shopping. I need to look like…her."

"This is about Ameana," Miku concludes.

"No. Well, not really. It's just that she is stunning all the time. I know I won't be that way but I want to be as beautiful and perfect as I can be. C'mon, Pretty, his last girl was a freaking angel!"

"So?"

"So that means she had a perfect angel body. Along with perfect angel breasts."

"You have breasts."

"Yeah, but they're not…done yet. I always thought they would get full and wonderful in a year or two. I don't know if you've heard, but I don't have a year."

"Don't worry. Whatever time doesn't give you, Victoria's Secret will."

"Okay, as long as it has lots of padding, 'cause…"

I study my chest in the mirror again.

"You keep doing that and you will never get Marcus to sleep with you."

"Doing what?"

"Comparing yourself to another girl. Guys hate that. You're amazing all on your own. You have to go in knowing that."

"You're right. I am fine. The way I dress is fine."

"Well…a little shopping couldn't hurt," she says softly.

"Will you go with me?"

"Sure."

"Thank you," I shout, hugging her tightly.

"Can I ask you another question?"

"So, we are officially not going to first period," Miku says to herself.

"This is much more important than math."

"What is it?"

"Did you get to have sex when you were human?"

"Yes."

"Did it hurt?"

"At first, then it got better."

"What did it feel like?"

"Strange, then nice, and then strange again; he wanted to do like a Q&A afterwards."

"Really?"

"Yeah. He was like 'How was I at this part?' 'Did I do this right?' 'How long should I have done that?'"

We burst out laughing. For the first time since I've known her, Miku is blushing.

"Then he launched into a bunch of random facts about the first time. It was like having sex with Wikipedia."

"So how would you rate his…?"

"Website?"

"Yeah."

"Not bad."

"How many guys have you…"

"Q&A guy and someone else."

"Did you love him?"

"Yeah, that's why it was better with him. I think sex is always better with the guy you love. Because even if it's bad, it's good."

"What about now, as an angel?"

"Sex for us is different."

"How?"

"Put it like this: Sex as a human is like a single firecracker. Sex as an angel is the Fourth of July."

"Wow…"

"I mean it, Emmy. You may not be able to handle it."

"But I want to try."

"Okay, then talk to Marcus. Just be up front with him."

"Do I need to buy condoms? Do angels need that?"

"Condoms are like cute shoes: you always need them. That is unless you're doing it with an angel. In that case, you two are fine."

"So there's no way I could get…"

"No."

"I don't understand why Marcus doesn't want to do it."

"He may be a little busy trying to save your life."

"Yeah, I guess. I just want us to have a night together that is perfect. I made a list."

"Of course you did."

I get up and take a small notepad out of my desk. I hand it to Miku. She begins to read it out loud.

"Flowers, music, candles…"

"I try to cover the basics. What do you think?"

"That's mostly for us. Guys just need one thing: the girl."

"I know I'm going overboard, but it's the memory I want to hold on to when…"

"You think Marcus is really going to take your life?"

"He doesn't have a choice."

"You are so brave, Em. I don't get to say that to you enough."

"I'm not really brave, actually. I just try to stay busy and not think about it. It got so bad the other day I actually studied for my chem test."

"Wow, you were desperate."

"Yeah and I got a B."

"Seriously?"

"Yup, leave it to me to become a super nerd just as my time runs out."

"When I was dying, I could only think of pain. But if I knew ahead of time, I'm not sure what my last thought would have been."

"Some days I think about serious stuff like what would college life have been like; what would my children have looked like; and other days I just think how much it sucks that I'm gonna miss the next installment of *The Hunger Games*."

Tears spring to my eyes. But I pull them back. I've gotten good at that. No more crying all the time. It does little to help. I look down at the floor. Miku places her hand over mine.

"Frat parties suck, someone always throws up on you. I hear childbirth is excruciating. And the books are always better than the movie."

"Well then, I'm totally ready for death now." I laugh despite myself. She looks at me with sadness and concern.

"Emmy, I'm sorry that you're…"

I know Marcus wants me to keep hoping, but when the girl that died the worst death in Guardian history looks up at you with that much pity… you know the end is very near.

It was a good thing Miku and I went shopping because a few days later, Marcus texted me. It turns out I didn't even need to seduce him.

"Hey, need 2 C U alone."

OMG! This is it! What do I do? What do I wear? How do I…should I…???

Okay, Emmy. Do. Not. Panic.

I make myself calmly reply to make sure that we are both on the same page.

"Is it about the Triplex?" I text.

"No. It's…personal."

Just to make extra sure, I text more questions.

"Will team B there?"

Please say "no."

"No."

We're going to have sex. Yes!

Wait. We're going to have sex?

OMG!!!

I sit on the edge of the bed and panic for a full five minutes. I have seen this stuff in movies all the time. Why is this still freaking me out? I have wanted this moment since I met him. There are a million butterflies doing a tumbling routine in my stomach.

I wish my mom was here. Well if she was, I'm sure she would be against it. In fact, she'd ground me forever, but still I could use a hug, or at the very least, antipsychotic meds because I am losing my mind.

"Okay, Emerson Hope Baxter, keep it together," I order myself out loud in the mirror.

"You have come a long way. You know he loves you. You love him. And tonight is going to be special. You're going to make love to an angel. How many girls get to say that?"

Then something happens that almost never happens: I talk myself out of panic mode. I walk over to the closet and pick out a black miniskirt and top Miku bought me. I put on heels and thank the heavens above that they are wedges. Had they not been, I would surely have fallen over. I let my hair out and put on some gloss. I'm not Ameana but I clean up pretty okay.

As I head out the door, my nerves give way to excitement. I love him so much. I can't wait for the chance to love him in a whole new way.

Jay and Rio are standing guard over me tonight. I didn't even have to call Rio for him to come and get me.

"I read your Wave: anxious and excited."

"Yeah," I say bashfully.

He reads more of my Waves.

"Oh, I see," he says.

"Rio, please don't tell anyone—"

"Hey, it's none of my business."

"How do I look?"

"Great."

"Thanks."

We head outside. Jay asks why I'm wearing a skirt. It's a fair question since I have made a religion out of jeans and sweaters. I say I just wanted to wear something different. He exchanges a look with Rio. This is so embarrassing.

I wish Marcus had come to pick me up himself. It would have been better if the whole team wasn't in on what was going on. But I don't even care at this point. All I want is to be alone with my boyfriend.

Once we get to the house, Rio and Jay see me upstairs and head back out. I enter and find Marcus among his books as usual. He looks up and sees me standing before him.

Suddenly I'm not really sure what to do with my hands. I keep shifting my weight and biting my lower lip. I think back on what Miku said and I try to give off an air of confidence.

"Hey," I say, in what I hope is a light, breezy, sexy tone.

"Hey," he says quickly.

"Where is everybody?" I ask, taking my coat off. I wait for him to see my new outfit.

"Demon hunting," he says, not looking up. Damn.

"Oh."

"That's why I asked you over."

"I kinda figured," I say slowly, gaining more confidence. He stands and gives me a quick kiss.

"I think it's about time this happened," he says softly in my hair.

"Okay, um…should we go to your room?" I ask, uncertain about undressing in the middle of the living room.

"No, out here is fine," he says simply.

"Okay." I want more privacy even though we are alone. But I don't want to disagree with him and ruin the mood.

"Stay right here," he says as he runs into his room.

I inhale deeply and prepare to be with the guy I love. As I stand there, my heart races and my hands shake. I go over it in my head. I will let him take the lead. That way, I can't go wrong.

Wait. Does he want *me* to take the lead?

Emmy, he's a Guardian. He's a natural-born leader. He will guide you. Now for once in your life, stop doubting yourself. Think about the last time you two made out. Think about how soft his lips felt pressed against yours. How you ached to be closer to him…

I take yet another deep breath and decide that I am done being scared. I am done being nervous. I have only weeks to live and I will not waste another moment in doubt.

I turn away, unbutton my blouse, and let it fall to the floor (just like they do in the movies). I stand there in a newly purchased black padded bra that enhances my chest by nearly a full cup. When I hear Marcus open the door, I whip around to face him and speak in my best grown-up voice.

"So, Mr. First Guardian, what do you think?"

Standing there with Marcus is Julian. Horrified, I desperately try to cover myself up with my hands. Shocked, Marcus runs to try to help me cover up.

Everything seems to be happening at once: Julian threatening to kill Marcus, me looking desperately for my blouse, and Marcus apologizing profusely.

I don't stop to address him. I don't even get my blouse. I just put my coat on and run out of the house. I don't want to wait for the New Year. Someone kill me now.

CHAPTER THREE: HELL IS EMPTY

"Will you let me in?" Marcus asks, pounding on my bedroom door. I don't answer. I stay under the covers and wait for some kind of merciful force to kill me…

Nothing happens.

Apparently Death takes his victims only when he's good and ready.

I've been home for an hour now. So far, I haven't been able convince time to back up and let me keep some of my dignity. How could it have gone so wrong? Why was Julian even there? I replay it over and over again. This experience is going to scar me for as long as I live.

Bright side: that'll only be for another seven weeks or so…

"You know I can just get in a Port and show up inside your room, right?" Marcus reminds me. I roll my eyes and open the door.

"Em, I didn't know that you thought tonight was…"

"I'm such an idiot!"

"It wasn't that bad."

"I stood in the middle of the living room half naked in front of Julian. Why was he even there?"

"He's really been on the edge since your mom died. I thought maybe it's time the two of you talked. That's why I had the team clear the house; so you guys could have some alone time."

"Julian isn't the one I needed alone time with," I mumble.

"I'm sorry I wasn't clear with you."

"Is that all you're sorry about?"

"Was there something else?" he asks, slightly irritated.

"You're not even a little sorry that we aren't going to be together tonight?"

"I want to be with you, you know that."

"How would I know, Marcus? By the way you spend hours away from me? Or the way you make plans to meet me, then send Rio instead?"

"You know what I'm trying to do here, Emmy."

"Upset me?"

"You misunderstood my text. That's not my fault."

"Why would you even bring Julian to the house? We have nothing to say to each other."

"You two need to talk."

"He's the reason we're all in this mess."

"I'm not a fan of the guy but the fact of the matter is, he's your father."

"So what?"

"You two have a connection."

"I can't believe you are standing here arguing on behalf of the man who raped my mom."

"Julian says—"

"I DON'T CARE WHAT HE SAYS!"

"He's trying to reach you."

"And I'm trying to reach *you*. Marcus, tonight was supposed to be… special. Now it's ruined."

"It's not ruined. You can still talk to your father."

"UGH!" I hurl my pillow at him. "You are not listening to me," I protest.

"No, Emerson, I hear you clearly. You want to push away the only family you have left."

"Why is it so important to you that I talk to Julian? He can't tell us anything new. He's useless to the mission now."

"Not everything is about the mission."

"This from the Guardian who spends twenty-six hours a day digging around in books?"

"I am not going to apologize for trying to save my girlfriend's life."

"I'm not gonna apologize for trying to get closer to you before I—"

I can't finish my thought. The room falls silent. Suddenly I'm aware of how I'm dressed. I had changed out of the nice clothes Miku got me.

I now have on pajama bottoms and a T-shirt featuring the forgetful fish from *Finding Nemo*. It reads "Just keep swimming."

Great, now we're alone, I have his undivided attention, and I'm dressed like I'm headed for a sleepover with Sponge Bob Square Pants…

"I know you're embarrassed but honestly, you standing in my living room half naked…I wouldn't take that back if I could."

I smile bashfully and turn away.

"I know I've been all work lately, but it doesn't mean I don't think about 'play,'" he insists.

"When you see us being together, who makes the first move?" I ask.

He answers me by wrapping his impossibly strong arms around me, carrying me over to the bed, and laying me down. Given the magnitude of his strength, I'm taken by the gentleness of his touch.

He longingly gazes down my body. It's as if he can see right through my clothes; in his mind's eye, I am naked. A moan escapes his slightly parted lips. He likes what he sees.

He kisses my fingertips, eyelids, and earlobe. He traces my jawline with his thumb, raises my head slightly, and nuzzles the nape of my neck. Nerve endings are ignited with every kiss he gives me. Once our lips finally meet, a chaos of warm sensation travels down my body.

The euphoria of his touch causes me to lose all sense of time and space. His kisses leave a trail of pleasure long after contact. My angel looks up at me as if to ask permission to take my shirt off. I signal that I'm ready. Then, his cell phone rings.

Damn…

I sigh heavily and lie back. Marcus, equally frustrated, answers.

"What?" he barks. He listens for a few seconds, then reluctantly agrees and hangs up.

"Who was that?" I ask.

"Your father. If you don't go talk to him, he's coming over here."

"Perfect," I reply, rolling my eyes.

Marcus laughs suddenly.

"What?" I ask.

"Your father calling and demanding you follow his rules, you with a guy in your room…for a second it feels like we are leading normal lives."

"Are you saying not everyone gets tortured and chased by Akons?"

"Hard to believe."

He takes my hand and we head back to the house where I was humiliated just a few hours ago. I would not have gone back, but Marcus pointed out that Julian was in fact very serious about coming over to my apartment if I didn't come see him.

It irritates me that Julian has decided to act like a father now. He has been absent for years and now he wants to run my life. I don't care what the council said or did. He was supposed to be there for me and he wasn't.

That isn't to say I would even want him here. I can't forgive what he did to my mom. Okay, maybe she was in love with him in some past life. But that doesn't make it right. And no matter how hard he tries, Julian will not be allowed to force his way into my life.

When we enter the Guardians' house, we find Julian and everyone but Rio waiting on us.

"We thought we'd stick around in case you guys came to blows," Miku says.

"My money's on Emmy. She's tapped into her abandonment issues. Lots of rage," Jay remarks.

Ameana shoots Jay a look that tells him this may not be the time to joke. She is right.

"Who are you to demand that I come and see you?" I ask Julian.

"After what I witnessed earlier, I see that you need help making good decisions," he retorts.

"Yo, what happened earlier?" Jay asks. I ignore him and address Julian.

"You freaking kidding me with this? You think you're the person to show me how to make good decisions? Let's see, what have you done that was so good? Oh yeah, you broke the council's rules, got my mom kicked out of the light, and then you raped her."

"You don't understand how much I loved your mother."

"When you love people, Julian, you support them and let them make their own decisions. Did you even ask my mother if she wanted your help finding her way into the light?"

"No."

"Of course not."

"I helped her get into the light."

"Yeah, then you helped her get kicked out. She has spent like a thousand Cycles here because you're a selfish bastard."

"Emmy—" Marcus starts.

"Let her continue," Julian replies.

"The truth is, I wish you never entered my mom's life."

"You don't have to…like me. But I am going to protect you any way I can."

Both of us start shouting at each other.

"QUIET!" Marcus shouts. The room falls silent immediately.

We were too deep in our argument to notice Rio had entered the room.

"Rio, what is it?" Marcus asks.

"They know the Triplex is inside Emmy."

"Who knows?"

"Everyone."

Everything happens in slow motion. I look out of the bay windows and see a slew of demons in the air, surrounding the house. They encircle the ground floor all the way up to the roof. The house is now at the center of a giant twister-like swirl of demons.

On the street below us, there is a motorcade of black SUVs that pull up to the front of the building. The car doors open, and an army of Runners and Pawns with guns make their way up the stairs.

Suddenly, cracks spread across the living room ceiling. Someone or something has landed on the roof. Just then, I spot the most beautiful birds making their way past the stream of demons. They are twice the size of bald eagles and made entirely of flames.

There's a peaceful glow that emanates from the awe-inspiring creatures. I can't take my eyes off their fiery wings. There's a beam of red light shining from their eyes, bringing with it a beauty too powerful to ignore. I could spend eternity looking at them. Suddenly they open their mouths. I await a magic, a wonder like none I have seen before. I reach out for it.

"Emmy, no!" Marcus tackles me to the ground. Just as we hit the floor the birds spew out a river of fire. The Guardians' home explodes into a massive ball of red and blue flames. Everyone and everything is catapulted into the sky.

The streets are littered with body parts and debris. The block where the house used to stand has been all but decimated. Marcus and I land several yards away. There's a dull pain traveling along the left side of my body and my head landed on the pavement, causing a massive migraine.

"Emmy!" he calls as he tries to stand up.

"I'm okay. Where are the others?"

"We're good!" Ameana says as she heads over to us along with the rest of the team.

"Jay, you have to get Emmy out. I don't have a Port on me."

"Can't," Jay replies. That's when we realize one of his wings has been badly injured.

"Jay, are your wings…?" Marcus asks.

"No, I'll survive, but for now, I can't Glide. Let alone fly."

"It's not a good idea to take to the air anyway, too many Fire Swans."

I look up in the sky and find the flaming birds still hovering above us. "Miku—"

"I can't sing, Marcus. There are too many Pawns here. They would all die."

From the corner of my eye, I spot Rage headed directly for us. The team spots him before I can even open my mouth. Rio quickly raises his shield a mere second before Rage sends a fireball our way. We can hear Rage laughing as New York City burns down.

"Give us the human!" he shouts as he attacks Rio's shield again.

"We have to move. The shield won't hold up!" Miku says.

"We can take to the sky long enough to escape to another country. We can regroup there," Jay says.

"No, they will follow and we can't let them harm any more humans," Marcus orders.

"We need to do something. I'm fading," Rio says between clenched teeth. As soon as he says that, Rage doubles his efforts by adding the Fire

Swans' blaze to his own. Together, the sea of fire is too much for Rio; his shield is down.

The instant that happens we are swarmed by demons, Pawns, Runners and Akons. It would be nothing for the angels to take out the Runners, but having Pawns in the mix slows things down. Since Pawns still have a soul, killing them is forbidden.

Ameana and Rio tackle demons to the left of me while Miku sings softly to a group of Runners. Marcus takes on the remaining Akons while trying to shield me from them. I have never seen a battle on this large a scale. Lucy has emptied hell and sent an army after me. All around, demons are getting their wings ripped off, Guardians struggle to gain control, and New York City burns.

"We'll hold them back. You make a run for it," Marcus instructs me.

I open my mouth to protest.

"No arguments. Go to the Sage. They won't attack you there. Run and don't look back."

Suddenly, I hear Rio cry out. I look over and a demon has plunged a metal rod right into his chest.

"Damn it, Emmy, RUN!" Marcus screams.

I take off down the street, my heart feeling like it's going to burst out of my chest with every step I take. I force myself to keep going although I desperately want to check on Rio and the others.

What if Rio is seriously hurt and Miku can't get there in time to heal him? What if Jay can't fend off the Akons because of his wings? Will Ameana and Miku be okay against so many demons all at once? And Marcus, one miscalculation, one misstep and his wings could end up spread on the White Mountain in Difi…

The picture of the morose mountain made of angel wings makes me queasy. My body pleads with me to slow down or better yet stop.

Emmy, keep going…

I order my legs to keep moving. The buildings go by me in a blur. I pay no attention to them or my screaming muscles. The burn inside my chest grows with every step I take, but I ignore that, too.

Then a few feet to the right of me, a man is set on fire. His cries fill the air. I look up and find Rage in the sky. He throws another fireball and the entire block goes up in flames. I run faster, but I know it's hopeless since I can't match his speed.

The only advantage I have over Rage is that it is against the rules for him to use his powers in a big crowd of humans. I look around anxiously for the most crowded street I can find. In New York City that isn't usually a problem but it wasn't even daybreak yet.

Finally, I spot a group of guys at a warehouse loading and unloading their trucks. I run right into the warehouse and pray there are a lot more people inside. Thankfully there is. I stand in the middle of the floor. Rage and I now stand separated by a crowd of humans.

Rage stands outside, just a few yards away from me. I can see from the look on his face, he's thinking about whether or not to take the risk.

"Rage, don't," I say breathlessly. The crowd starts asking each other what's going on.

Rage looks into my eyes.

"So, you really have it in there, don't you?"

I don't respond. He doesn't need to know I'm scared. He doesn't need to know that at any moment my legs are going to give out on me.

"We're going to get it from you. We will tear into your flesh and pop out your eyeballs," he says with a sweet smile.

"Maybe. But not today."

He sneers at me and leaves. I'm so weak with relief, I sit on the ground and hold my head between my hands.

One of the workers comes up to me and asks if I'm okay.

"Yes, thank you."

He holds out his hand and helps me up.

"Was that guy your boyfriend?"

"No."

"Good, I can tell from his face—he's no angel."

I shake my head and smile at the biggest understatement of the century. Once the sun comes up and the streets are filled with humans, I make my way to the Sage's place. I am careful not to use any side streets or wander anywhere that's isolated. By the time I get to the Sage, it's nearly eight in the morning.

I knock on the door and the old lady with the kind face, whose name we don't know, lets me in. I don't even get a foot in the door when Marcus moves in to hug me.

"I was gonna come look for you but we didn't want to lead the Akons to you," he explains.

I don't have any words. I just want to stay in his arms, but a thought jolts me out of Marcus's embrace.

"Is Rio okay?" I ask.

"Yeah, I healed the crybaby," Miku says.

"What? I healed you just last week when a demon broke your legs."

"It was just one leg and that took like ten seconds."

As the twins bicker on, I ask about Jay and Julian. Marcus tells me they are in Daraquin getting treated but that they should be fine.

"We should take you there and have them look at you," he says.

"I'm okay."

He shakes his head but lets the subject go. Just seeing his beautiful face again, knowing that he's standing there in front of me and not sprawled out on the sidewalk, dead…

I grab him and hug him again, as tight as I can. I whisper quietly in his ear and ask him to make a promise a leader fighting evil can never make.

"Don't die, okay?" I ask softly.

He looks into my eyes and sees them swimming in tears.

"I won't," he swears.

"Promise?"

"Promise."

I put my head on Marcus's chest. I spot the Sage standing at the doorway. His expression is that of a boy who has read ahead in a story and knows it won't end well. I turn and face the other way.

CHAPTER FOUR: PHIN

"We can't stay here, can we?" I ask.

"No. The Sage isn't supposed to be taking sides," Marcus confirms.

"So why is he helping us?"

"It's not because he likes me, that's for sure."

The twins and Ameana enter the tea room. It seems that every time we get life-altering news, it's here. The Sage has decorated the room with plush furniture, a magnificent tea set, and a chessboard made out of pieces that represent Akons and Guardians.

Marcus hates the tea room. To him, it is the place where we found out that Hun, an ancient evil, was alive and well. For me, this room is where we found out that Rio was alive. It is also in this room that Marcus said he loved me out loud. So naturally, the tea room holds a certain comfort.

"We can't just hide out here," Ameana says.

"I know. I'm thinking," Marcus replies.

"Thinking about what?" the twins ask in unison. They have been doing that a lot more. It kind of creeps me out, but I guess after all they have been through, they feel a closeness none of us will ever know.

"I'm trying to figure a way out of this," Marcus replies, clearly annoyed.

"We've looked for months, Marcus," Ameana insists.

"Yes, and we'll keep looking," he vows.

"The Akons aren't going to stop until they get Emmy," Miku says.

"So I should just kill her here and now?" Marcus snaps.

"Um…I'm gonna head to the kitchen. This sounds like team business," I say, closing the door behind me. The Sage is waiting for me in the hallway. I guess he knew I would be there.

"Naturally," he says out loud.

"That 'reading minds' thing, does it ever get old?"

"Not yet," he replies.

Well, it's getting old with me…

I make my way to the kitchen. Much like the rest of the apartment, the kitchen is spotless and cozy. From the tan checkered dish towels to the embroidered pot holders that say "Home." There is a painting on the wall of a roaring fireplace with a sweet-natured old lady sitting beside it, sipping from a mug.

I go to make myself some tea but it's already been made for me. The Sage had it sitting out waiting for me. It's peppermint, my favorite. That's what I always want to drink when I am at the Sage's house, peppermint tea. It goes well with whatever revelations he's going to share with us.

"There is no revelation this time, Emerson. If you live, many will die," he says, reading my thoughts once again.

"Don't you ever get tired of being inside my head?"

"No, you are very entertaining."

"I do what I can."

He invites me to sit down at the table. I take a seat as he studies me.

"You are managing well for a girl whose love is supposed to kill her," he says.

"Um…thanks?"

"Marcus has wanted to ask you a question for weeks now."

"Whatever it is, he'll tell me when he's ready."

"Marcus isn't ready for anything. He's in love. He's lost."

"Is that what it means to be in love?"

"At this moment, yes."

"He wants to find a way to save me. That's what angels do."

"He's a Guardian. He has a mission."

"I tried to tell him but he won't listen to me."

"You don't know what's at stake, Emerson. You will bring about the end of everything."

"It's not my fault. The council did that."

"They hid the map and gave the clue as to its location. Their job is done."

"This isn't fair."

"You have been with the Guardians for nearly a year. You know all their Cores, yet you still believe the universe deals in fairness?"

"I'm not a fan of dying, okay? But if I have to, why does it have to be Marcus that does it?"

"It doesn't have to be. It could be Lucy."

"Those are my only choices?"

"You know very well it is. That is what you have been trying to convince Marcus of for all this time."

"Yeah and you can see how well that's working."

"He would die for you."

"I know."

"But it is not his life he is risking. It is the humans."

"What am I supposed to do?"

"Help him see what he's unwilling to look at."

He shouldn't have to make this decision. We should be in school, taking exams, cutting class, kissing in the hallways...

"From what I understand, the two of you have found time to get the kissing part in," he says.

Can I have one thought to myself, please?

"Apologies," he says.

I lean forward in my chair, close my eyes, and rub my temple.

"The mailman dropped off a package. I believe it's a Phin," someone says.

I open my eyes and find the old lady who hardly ever speaks standing at the doorway. She leaves the kitchen before I can ask any questions. I turn my attention to the Sage.

"What does that mean?"

"It means we have a visitor."

We head to the entrance of the apartment, where the team examines the contents of the package that had just been delivered.

Marcus reaches inside the small cardboard box and pulls out an ivory colored bottle with a carving on the side. The carving is of the number 3, and alongside it is the letter C, which link together to form a spade.

"What is that and where's the visitor?" I ask.

"Inside," Marcus says.

"It has your name on it," Ameana says to him.

"An angel's wings are like human fingerprints, each is unique. Since Marcus's name is on the box, only feathers from his wings can make open it," Rio explains.

Then Marcus calls for a feather from his wings. It flows into the air and then runs along the side of the bottle. Suddenly a dark shadow seeps out of the bottle. It forms into an older man dressed in what looks like a butler's uniform.

"A genie?" I shout, before I can stop myself.

"I beg your pardon, madam?" the figure says with a heavy British accent.

"You're some type of genie, right?"

"Emmy, there are no such things as genies," Miku says.

"But he came in a bottle, for Omnis's sake."

"I beg your pardon, madam, but that isn't a bottle; it's a Phin," he informs me.

"A Phin is a vehicle that houses Shadow Servants," Rio explains.

"Humans have a myth about beings that come out of bottles and grant wishes," Miku explains to the figure.

"I am aware of the humans' offensive portrayals of Shadow Servants," he says, sounding less than happy with us.

"I've met Shadow Servants before but they were wrapped around a tree, greeting guests for a party. I didn't know they also delivered messages. So I thought maybe you were a...sorry," I reply.

The Shadow Servant looks down at me.

"Yes, well, my name is Lakom. I am a Shadow Servant from The House of Three. I am not a genie. I do not grant wishes and you will not rub me."

It was all the Guardians could do not to laugh. I would have thought it funny too, if Lakom didn't look like he wanted to strangle me for offending him.

"What is your message?" the twins ask.

"My message is for Marcus Cane. The First Guardian of the current Cycle."

"I'm Marcus."

"My Maker wishes to speak with you and your team."

"Who is your Maker?"

"The head of The House of Three."

Marcus looks around, and like him, the team has no idea what Lakom is talking about.

"Sage, do you know The House of Three?" Marcus asks.

"No."

"Nevertheless, she wishes to meet with you."

"Why should we go see her?"

"Because she is the answer."

"The answer to what?"

"Everything."

Lakom dissolves into a shadow again, leaps out and up into the light fixtures, and disappears.

That is so cool…

Marcus takes the Phin and reads a message engraved on the side:

"Terra Oblivioni.
First light.
Seek: Lakom"

"Judging from the reaction of the team, I'm guessing Terra Oblivioni isn't a place for fun and laughs," I say to Miku.

"It's 'The Land of the Forgotten,'" she explains.

Rio, reading my Waves, knows I'm still confused. He tries to explain further.

"Terra is home to most if not all Tics."

"You mean it's filled with bugs?" I ask.

"No, Tic is another word for an angel who's addicted to drugs."

"Drugs?"

"There's two major drugs that plague the Angel world: Peeks and CP. Peeks are black market Snaps that last for hours instead of a few minutes. Angels get a high from the new power they have. Unfortunately, no matter how strong the Peek is, the high is temporary. So they have to buy more. Peek Snaps are expensive; they come from the third layer of our wings."

"That's the layer that can't grow back."

"Yes."

"So the angels get hooked on Peeks and end up depleting their entire third coat?"

"Eventually."

"And without their third coats—"

"They can't fly. They're Grounded; earthbound forever."

"What's CP?" I ask.

"Coy Paste," Miku says.

"You guys drink Coy though, right?"

"Yes, but the liquid form is fine. It is exceedingly more potent in paste form. Angels smear it on their wings. It gives them a blissful, all-consuming surge. Like Peeks, the rush from CP is also temporary and depletes the third coat."

"Why do angels risk their wings just for a rush?" I ask.

"Same reasons humans risk their lives," Marcus says, bitterly reflecting on his mom.

"Once an angel is Grounded, he'll do anything to get his hands on more Peek or CP. The council found addicted angels were dangerous. So they banished them to Terra. It's a small strip of land near New Jersey."

"Can we skip the Q&A and focus? We can't just accept the invitation," Ameana says.

"She's right. We can't just go to Terra to see some girl. What if it's a trap set by the Akons or Lucy?" I reply.

"Lucy can't enter Terra. She's banned. She doesn't really care anyway. She knows eventually Tics will overdose and end up in Difi."

Just then Jay Glides into the room with Julian. Thankfully, his wings have been repaired. And Julian doesn't have a scratch on him. Julian doesn't say anything but he looks me over carefully. There is a small breath of relief once he realizes that I'm in one piece. We catch Jay up on what he's missed.

"So, are we going to Terra?" he asks.

"Julian, have you ever heard of The House of Three?" Marcus asks.

"No, but if it's located in Terra, it can't be good. It's a wasteland of addicts and degenerates."

Marcus confers with the Sage.

"It is not for me to say. I can only point out that time is not your friend," the Sage says softly.

"He's right, Marcus. I broke a Splash when we were in Daraquin; the Akons, Runners, demons, and Lucy are all hunting for Emmy. Lucy has vowed to reward whoever finds her."

"What's the reward?" Rio asks.

"I don't know, a lifetime supply of evil in a can."

"Evil in a can?" Miku mocks.

"Yo, whatever. All I know is they are coming for her hard."

"So, are we going?" I ask nervously.

"Yeah," Marcus says, without missing a beat.

"Are you sure this is a good move?" Ameana asks.

"It may not be a *good* move, but it's our only one."

Marcus instructs the team to go Recharge and be ready to move out in a few hours. As they head off to find a place to rest, I hear Jay address Ameana.

"I saw your man," Jay teases.

"Excuse me?" Ameana says.

"Please, like you don't know who I mean."

"I don't."

"Well, *Wolf* said he's been calling you, but you don't pick up."

"We've been a little busy here. You know, saving the world?"

"Whatever, man, just call that dude back."

"So what, you two are best friends now?"

"If we were cool like that, I'd tell him to stay away from you. I have met girls that require a few hours of work, but you are trouble 3-6-5."

"So you told him how awful I am and he still wanted you to get a message to me?"

"All I can do I warn a guy, ya know?"

"I didn't call him because I'm on a mission. I don't have time to socialize."

"Too bad your ex does."

Chapter Four: Phin

Flashes of anger flood Ameana's face. She raises her hand and sends Jay flying through the window and across the street. We turn around in time to hear Jay shout.

"I'm good. The kid is always good," Jay shouts from across the street. I can hear the smile in his words. He's having a good time teasing Ameana.

Marcus shakes his head impatiently and the twins head out to get Jay.

"Has Wolf been calling you?"

"Who's asking? The First Guardian or my ex?"

"Your friend."

"Are we friends?" She laughs joylessly.

"We used to be."

"We used to be a lot of things, Marcus." She walks off, but he takes after her.

They enter the tea room. It's all I can do not to go over and put my ear to the door.

That would be wrong, right?

Right.

Luckily, their voices carry down the hallway.

Emmy, it's a private conversation. You should walk away. Be a good girlfriend and walk away. Walk away. Emmy, move!

I don't budge.

Do eavesdroppers ever make it into the light? Yeah, didn't think so.

I hear Marcus speak first.

"Things don't have to be this way between us."

"What way?" she asks.

"We don't have to be enemies."

"We're not. We're coworkers."

"Seriously?"

"I really don't know what you want me to say."

"Say that we can be friends."

"What difference does that make?"

"How can you ask that? What is wrong with you? Why are you acting like this? Are you really this mad because we broke up?"

"You really don't get it."

"No, Ameana, I don't. Explain it to me."

"You didn't leave me the night you broke up with me. You left me months before that but you were too much of a coward to admit it."

"I was honest with you."

"Liar! Every laugh we shared, every kiss you gave me after you laid eyes on Emmy was a lie."

"What we had—"

"What we had was over. But instead of telling me, you spent weeks pretending. I kept thinking I was doing something to push you away. I blamed myself for not being a good girlfriend to you."

"It's not your fault we broke up. You have to know that."

"Breaking up is what decent guys do. They fall for another girl, admit it, and make a clean break. That's not what you did."

"What did I do?"

"YOU ABANDONED ME!!!"

A heavy silence fills the apartment. When Ameana speaks again, she is calm and in control. But there's a sadness in her tone that betrays her attempts to appear composed.

"I loved you. You loved me. Something changed. You should have told me. I deserved to know. Instead you let me be in it alone. Marcus, how could you let me be in love alone?"

A few hours later, we prepare to leave the Sage's home and head for Terra. Although everyone Recharged, they don't look very rested. I think not knowing what they are headed for has everyone on edge.

While the team pours over a map of Terra, I grab a breakfast of toast and tea from the kitchen. The Sage offers to have the old lady make eggs, but I have learned the hard way that it's best to eat light when you are traveling with Guardians.

As we head out the door, the Sage stops us. His voice is serious and filled with sorrow.

"I would like to think we are all friends," he says.

We all exchange a look but don't say anything.

"It pains me to know the truth. Still I feel it only fair to share it with you," he continues.

"What is it?" Marcus asks.

"I do not foresee all of you returning. In fact, I guarantee it."

CHAPTER FIVE: HOUSE OF THREE

We arrive in Terra Oblivioni, a few miles outside of New Jersey. There is nothing here but abandoned warehouses and dilapidated buildings. They told me it would be filled with drug-addicted angels but nothing they said could have prepared me for this heart-wrenching sight.

The Tics look more like zombies than angels. In truth, I'm not sure the things sticking out of their backs can even be called wings. They look more like the skeleton of what *used* to be wings. The disturbing and sad sight makes me flinch.

Each Tic has wing damage but to different degrees. There is a Tic propped up alongside an abandoned car; his feathers are gone. There's only a thin layer preventing us from seeing the skeleton of his wings.

Other Tics don't even have the skeleton intact. One Tic over by the trash can has only two bones protruding out of his shoulder blades.

"What happened to him?" I ask Jay.

"Sometimes when a Tic runs out of feathers, he'll break off a piece of his wing bone and sell it for drugs."

"His bones are worth something?"

"Angel bones look like humans' but they aren't. They are vastly stronger and more valuable. When angel bone is ground up and mixed with other ingredients, it has a number of uses. Many of the items sold in the market consist of angel bone," Rio explains.

I am unable to take my eyes off the Tics roaming aimlessly in the streets. What I find even more disturbing than the Tic's wings is the state of their bodies. They are severely underweight. They stagger out into the streets like drunks with no equilibrium.

At first it looks like they are zombies with black and grey polka dots for skin. But then Marcus tells me the black dots are splotches where darkness has invaded their soul. I look into their eyes and a cold chill runs down my body. There is a black void where their eyes used to be. Miku says they can still see us, it's just that the light has been drained from their eyes.

Some Tics are missing fingers and other body parts. I'm told that's because some attempt to sell off as much of themselves as possible for just one more hit of Peek or CP.

Their bodies are so frail, it's as if death haunts their every step. There is no way to really tell the males from the females since most of them are bald. The decay of their souls is reflected in every inch of their bodies.

"Shouldn't we help them?" I ask.

"There is no helping a Tic," Marcus informs me.

"Technically they can kick the habit," Miku says, uncertain.

"Yeah, and Sellers make it into the light. Give me a break." Marcus snorts.

I look up at the Guardians and their radiant wings flying against the still air.

"So, if angel feathers are what they need to get more drugs, then you guys—"

Rio finishes my thought. "We are a major payday for them."

"Exactly why we need to find Lakom before—" Marcus never gets to finish his sentence.

A few yards away from us, a Tic grunts out a series of loud noises. The entire town of Terra never realized we were there until then. At once, every single Tic registers our presence by turning towards us.

"Why didn't they see us before?" I ask.

"It's like they are sleepwalking when they're under the influence. But sooner or later, one of them comes back to reality, if only for a short time," Miku says.

"That's when they realize there are angels among them," Jay says.

"I'm guessing that's bad," I say, almost to myself.

"Very bad," Rio confirms.

Suddenly, every Tic in Terra is headed our way. It only takes seconds for the mob of zombie angels to surround us. It looks like a scene out of a bad Halloween flick. The teens are eaten by a mob of flesh-eating monsters. But in the movies, you can fast-forward the parts that scare you. We will not have that luxury.

The Tics force us into the center of the mob. There are hundreds of them. They grunt and howl like animals.

"We can take them," Marcus says.

"Yes, but should we?" Miku asks.

"Should we? Hell yeah we should!" Jay whispers to us.

"I'm just saying they are angels just like us. They have souls," Miku explains.

"I don't care if they have my grandmother's eyes and my mama's meatloaf recipe. We take 'em down," Jay insists.

"The soul argument is a little weak, Pretty; they barely have any soul left," Ameana replies.

"That's not the point."

"Well, when is an angel not really an angel anymore?" Rio asks.

"That sounds like a great topic. Maybe we could get it to trend on Twitter later. But right now, can we just find a way out?" I ask.

"We can't hurt them, Marcus. I won't," Miku insists.

The Tics study the Guardians' wings as if they're too good to be true. Marcus takes my hand and places me behind him. I could point out that since I don't have wings, I'm no danger but then again, they ripped their own body parts off...

"Can you use your shield?" Marcus asks Rio.

"They're too close," Rio replies.

"They weak, man, we got this," Jay says.

"What they lack in strength they make up for in desperation. The last time I underestimated an addict, she killed me," Marcus warns.

He then signals to Ameana. Before I can get a handle on what's happening, a rust-infested car cuts through the air and heads straight into the crowd. The Tics try to get out of the way but many don't make it in time.

The team tries to take to the air but nothing happens. Rio says it's a no-fly zone and we have to make a run for it. We turn back and find that

Tics, no matter how drugged out, don't care to be attacked. We have now pissed off the entire town of Terra.

They run after us with renewed dedication. They take off in speeds I didn't think they were capable of. We bolt down the street.

"We need to take them out, Marcus," Jay says.

"No, we aren't killing our own," Miku protests.

"Look at them, Miku; they have no issues taking us out."

"I'm not singing to them," Miku vows.

"They're trying to kill us. C'mon, yo!" Jay says, frustrated.

"Then Glide away, whatever," Miku retorts

"I'm not gonna Glide and leave my team."

"How can they run this fast?" I ask.

"They know if they catch us, it will buy them an unlimited supply of drugs," Rio says.

Seconds later, a Tic gets close enough to Jay. He lunges into the air and drags Jay down to the floor. Within seconds, half a dozen Tics invade Jay's body. The team fights to pull them off. They aren't strong, but the sheer number of the mob makes it difficult for the team to get a good handle on the situation.

The Tics are like bees. One of them is easy to take care of, but when they number in the hundreds, they are deadly. The Tics leap on top of the Guardians, a dozen to each member. They pull, claw, and bite their way towards the Guardians' wings.

The Guardians fling Tics to the left and right but the more they fend off, the more come back. Then a voice speaks with a heavy British accent:

"Perhaps I could be of service, madam?"

"Lakom!" I turn and find my favorite "not a genie" standing a few yards away.

"The Port has been preprogrammed," he says, pointing to awaiting Ports.

I call Marcus's attention to the Ports. Marcus instructs the team to go ahead while he takes care of the Tics. The team makes their way to the Ports.

Marcus uses a street lamp from the ground and turns it into a makeshift bat. He is able to keep the mob away but not for long. Soon they invade again, this time willing to die just to get to him.

"Hurry!" I scream.

Marcus is already on the run. The Tics take off after him. Rio holds out his hand and pulls Marcus up just in time. The last thing we see is the mob turning on each other.

The once strong and powerful angels, who used to battle evil, now battle for two stray feathers on the ground.

Traveling in a Port is as quick as blinking. One moment you're in one place, then you open your eyes, and you are somewhere completely different. I'm not sure what I expected to see after seeing the mob of zombie angels, but I certainly didn't expect to see what stands before us.

The team and I are transported to the center of a glorious Japanese garden. It's the kind of place you see in travel shows and it makes you ache to be there. Every single thing in this garden is perfect.

There are bonsai trees throughout the garden with shades of green so vivid, it's impossible not to stare. But you are forced to look away because there is yet another fantastic sight your eyes long to behold: the flowers. The impossible beauty emanating from them makes the garden feel like what I feel when I'm around Marcus: Calm. Peaceful. Loved.

The wind blows gently, causing the leaves to swan dive gracefully off the trees and into the pond below. On the surface of the pond are leaves and flower petals that have met a similar joyous fate, thanks to the cool breeze. The only sound comes from the steady flow of water streaming from the top of the waterfall as it merges into the pond.

The focal point of the garden is a bright red bridge that goes over the water; a few yards past the bridge is a pathway that leads to a Japanese-style temple. On the front of the temple there is a red carving just like the one on the Phin. It's the number 3 and alongside it is the letter C, linked to make the shape of a spade.

Chapter Five: House of Three

Honestly, I don't care what is in the temple. I just want to stay here in this garden of unimaginable beauty. This would be the perfect place to spend my last few weeks. I wonder if I can get Marcus to agree to it.

Yeah, right. I could just see how that conversation would go:

Me: Hey, why don't we stay in this amazing, peaceful place until it's time for me to die?

Marcus: No.

Me: But—

Marcus: No.

Me: Nothing is going to stop me from having to die, so let's stay here and have fun until it's time.

Marcus: No.

"Emmy? Hello?" Rio says.

"Oh, sorry; spaced out," I reply, shaking my head.

"You spaced out? Shocking," Ameana says, mildly irritated.

"I was just thinking how beautiful this place is."

"It's lovely," Miku agrees.

I look over at Marcus and take a shot.

"Maybe you and I could stay here for a while," I suggest.

"No."

Do I know my boyfriend or what?

Lakom tells us to follow him. It's strange but when he speaks it feels wrong to do anything but follow his instructions. It's like being in grade school and having the teacher tell me what to do. It never occurs to me to disobey.

Still, I would love to just sit in this garden with Marcus. We would finally get a chance to talk. I would get to ask the thing I've never really had time to ask him. I have always wanted to know more about his family on Earth. I would love to know more about his mom and what his life was like before he died.

"We are now in The House of Three?" Jay asks.

"Yes," Lakom replies as we make our way up the stone front steps of the temple.

We enter what looks to be the center of the temple. There is a slightly elevated platform that has three enormous throne-like chairs, made of some kind of black rock. The room is almost empty. There is nothing in here aside from the three thrones and a wall of water cascading behind it.

"Am I the only one thrown by this?" Rio asks.

"No, it doesn't make sense. Are we still in Terra?" Ameana wonders.

"No. You are in The House of Three in the City of Adam."

We follow the voice and find a beautiful girl about our age sitting on the throne in the center. She has rosy cheeks, plum-red, heart-shaped lips, and piercing blue eyes. Her hair is silver and shimmers like the sun reflecting on the pond in the garden.

She pulled her luminous hair into a bun high on top of her head. There isn't one strand out of place. She wears a simple, nude-color dress made of silk. It complements her complexion but clashes with the hardness of the throne.

Judging from her frame and her posture, I would say she's had years of ballet training. But with angels, that's just how they are, naturally graceful. That's why I am so shocked by what I see in front of me. Or, should I say, what I don't see.

"Where are her wings?" I ask Marcus under my breath.

"Good question," he replies.

Could she be human?

"Marcus, I apologize. I did not arrange anywhere for you and your team to sit. I was unsure what state you would be in when you arrived. The Tics can be—unkind to angels. I thought perhaps you and your team would be in need of Recharging."

"We're fine. We would like to know who you are and why you have summoned us here."

"Lakom, you can go. Thank you."

Lakom nods slightly, leaps into the nearest light fixture, and disappears.

"We have much to go over. Please have a seat," she says.

Just as the words leave her mouth, a row of plush armchairs appear.

Okay, so she's not human because she has powers. But she has no wings, so she's not an angel. What the hell is she?

Looking around the room, I am not the only one who's perplexed by this.

"If this is not to your liking, perhaps this will work?" she says as the armchairs are replaced by wooden chairs with carvings. Marcus ignores the chairs and addresses the girl.

"What are you?"

"I am Quo."

"What is that?" the twins ask.

"I will answer all of your questions. However, it is my turn," she addresses Marcus.

"You are on a search to save both your love and your mission. A search, I understand, that is about to fail."

Rio reads Marcus's Waves and signals to me that he doesn't like what he sees.

"What the hell is it you want?" Marcus snaps.

The quickest way to piss off my favorite angel is to tell him he's going to fail at saving me.

"You have come all this way. Have a seat and we will talk," she says pleasantly.

Marcus exchanges glances with the rest of the team and they're all in agreement. We take a seat on the wood chairs.

As soon as we do, a table appears before us. Then glasses filled with Coy appear.

"Please, help yourselves," she says. Marcus shoots her an impatient look. She smiles.

"I understand. It is difficult to wait. We have waited a long time and we are familiar with the torture that accompanies the act."

"So end the waiting and tell us what this is about," Ameana demands.

"My name is Chance. I am the leader of the Quo people."

"And what are the Quo people exactly?" I ask, before Marcus can bark at her again.

"I promise to answer your question shortly. For now, I would like to ask a question of your leader. Marcus, I have heard you have taken to reading fairytales in order to remove the Dy that's been cast into your love. Is that true?"

"Yeah," he says, slightly embarrassed.

"You have been looking into the story of Isis and Demetri?"

Marcus stands up and eagerly addresses Chance.

"Do you know something? Is there really an Amulet or did Lucy destroy it? I know it's just a story but I was hoping the Amulet part was true. Is it?"

"It is not a fairytale. The story is true."

All of us at the table exchange a glance. Marcus is in such a hurry, he stumbles over his words.

"Wait, are you sure—how do you—why are you—"

"Stop it!" I shout at Chance. My voice echoes in the room. Everyone turns towards me.

"Look, I'm sorry but it's not fair to keep Marcus hoping for something that's never going to come. I have read the story of Isis and Demetri a million times. It's just a story. There were no star-crossed lovers. No blue rain. No Amulet."

"Emmy, calm down," Miku says.

"No. Look, Prima Ballerina, I'm not gonna let you mess with the people I love by giving them false hopes. If the story was true, it would mean that Lucy killed Demetri. That means she also destroyed the Amulet. It's time everyone just accepted the fact that I'm going to die."

"C'mon, baby girl, everything's gonna be fine—" Jay starts.

"It's not. I have to die. That sucks but at least I have a few weeks. Why can't everyone just leave things alone and let me enjoy the time I have left?"

Marcus's face falls. Looking at his expression makes my heart sink. He wanted so much for there to be another way. I get up and take his hand.

"I'm sorry," I whisper to him quietly.

He can't bring himself to look at me.

"Will you please allow the 'ballerina' to finish?" Chance says.

"Rio, is she lying?" Marcus asks.

"No, but she does have secrets," he replies.

"I never said I didn't," Chance retorts.

"Let her finish," Jay says.

"As I was saying, the story is real. But at the same time, the story is untrue."

"I don't get it," Miku says.

"Demetri and Isis did fall in love. They did have triplets and the council did tempt Demetri with infinite power. What isn't known is that the Amulet contained nothing. The council had tricked Demetri."

"Great, so this guy killed his three daughters for nothing," Jay says, clearly disgusted.

"Demetri was a smart demon. He was sure the council would never give him that kind of power. Still he wanted to see what was inside. When he was finally able to open the Amulet, there was no power to be found."

"So, even if the story was true, there's nothing in the Amulet," Marcus says, mostly to himself.

"Yes, but he was victorious in that he was able to open it."

"He had to kill his daughters, how is that victory?" I ask.

"His daughters are alive and well."

"How do you know?" Marcus asks.

"I am one of them." She smiles sweetly and signals off to the side. Just then two other girls appear on the elevated platform. Aside from different hairstyles, all three of them look exactly alike.

"This is my middle sister, Choice," Chance says.

Choice's shining silver hair frames her perfect face and cascades down her back. Judging from the smirk on her face, she is enjoying the attention as she takes her seat on the throne beside her sister.

"And this is my youngest sister, Charity."

Charity is a carbon copy of her older sisters, except her silver hair is in a mass of shimmering, loose curls. She is biting her nails as she heads to her throne. She never looks up at us, only at the floor. Once they are all seated, Chance addresses us.

"We are the daughters of Isis and Demetri. As you can see, our father cast the Dy out of us safely. We will show you how to do the same for the one you love. The question, First Guardian, is this: if we help you, will you help us?"

"I will give you anything," Marcus vows, still shocked at the sight of the triplets.

Bemused, Chance answers him.

"No, Guardian. We don't require *anything* from you. We require *everything*."

CHAPTER SIX:
ADAM CITY

"My father was worried that we weren't born with wings. He thought maybe they would appear later. That was not the case. As the years went on, we simply never gained the ability to fly. My father was certain we were cursed by the council for the actions he and my mother took.

"Then one day, he stumbled onto this area and was shocked to discover that his daughters weren't the only ones who had powers but no wings. Thousands of beings were created the same way.

"It was then he uncovered the secret that the council had been hiding: humans and angels have been mating for several Cycles. Their offspring are angel/human hybrids called Quo. The council feared the Quos would put the world off balance. In addition, they didn't want breeding between angel and human to become common practice.

"So they cast the Quo people out here, only miles from the violence and lawlessness of Terra. Our family is the only one to have had wingless children born of two winged beings. That made us much talked about. In addition, my father helped build the city and worked tirelessly on behalf of the Quo people.

"So when it came time to elect a leader, naturally they chose him. My father had a best friend and advisor. The advisor became known as the Godfather of Adam City. Together the two of them built a thriving place where outcasts were made to feel welcomed. They raised us to believe that even though the council had deserted us, we were not worthless.

"They instilled in us the notion that we are only as limited as our minds. There is nowhere wings can take us that sheer determination cannot.

Together they were strong, resourceful, intelligent beings. They led us for many Cycles.

"The council put a Trimeter at the entrance of Adam City. This was done long before our family came to live here. The Trimeter reads our DNA. No one who is Quo can leave Adam City. For years my father and Godfather tried to find a way to free us. It took them many Cycles, but finally they were able to combine the right mixture to fool the Trimeter. They poured the mixture into the Amulet for safekeeping and planned on freeing the city the next day.

"Unfortunately, my father became seriously ill. We did all we could to tend to him. Godfather was beside himself with worry. The entire city prayed for their ruler's health and well-being. But nothing worked. Soon, my father was stricken with a serious case of dementia.

"He believed everyone around him was out to destroy him. In his confused state, he put the Amulet on a Port and sent it to parts unknown. He did this thinking no harm would come to him so long as he was the only one who knew where it was. The illness took my father's life before we were able to find where he had sent the Amulet.

"Godfather was able to come up with another mixture; unfortunately, it was too weak. It was only able to fool the Trimeter long enough to get him out. He has been in search of the Amulet with the original mixture for many Cycles now. While he is away, I am leading the Quo people. Although he is not here with us, Godfather has never forgotten us. He has labored and risked everything to set us free.

"Finally all of his hard work has brought us to this moment. Godfather has located the Amulet. It's in a place that is too treacherous for him to travel. We would like you and your team to go on his behalf and get it."

"Where is it?" Marcus asked.

"In the Pyron fields."

"That means the Amulet is with—"

"Yes. The Amulet is with Kairo."

I know in my soul I will have nothing but regret when I ask the team this question…

"Who's Kairo?"

"The only demon angels are forbidden to kill," Jay informs me.

"Why can't you guys kill him?"

"Politics," Marcus says bitterly.

"I don't understand."

"The council worries killing him will make them look as if they are showing favoritism towards good. Also killing Kairo would severely enrage Lucy, causing her to be even more destructive."

"Why does Lucy care so much about Kairo?"

"He's her son."

Like I said: nothing but regret.

"Um…no one ever told me Lucy had a son!"

"She didn't give birth to him, she created him. The two of them had a falling out and she banished him to Pyron."

"Okay, so how bad is this Kairo guy?"

"Kairo is—"

"Nothing to worry about," Marcus lies. I know he's lying because the others are exchanging quick, worried glances with each other.

"You're saying there is a whole race of people that the council has been hiding?" Rio asks.

"Yes, we have been held here."

"Why would you want to leave this place? It's beautiful," I volunteer.

"It's a prison!" the middle sister snaps. We all turn to look at Choice. There's a sort of frenzy behind her eyes.

"Forgive her, Choice can be rather tempestuous," Chance confesses.

"It's okay," I say awkwardly.

"Once you have obtained the Amulet and bring it to us, we will cast the Dy out of the human," she assures Marcus.

"When you're free, what do you plan to do?" Jay asks.

"Many of us will remain here in Adam City."

"Then what's the point?" Jay pushes.

"The point is we are beings like any other and we have the right to choose where we live," Chance says clearly, with an ice-cold certainty.

"Chance is very passionate about our freedom. She can be a lot to take," the youngest, Charity, offers gently.

"Who is this Godfather? We need to speak with him," Marcus says.

"He only speaks to those whom he wishes. You do not summon him. He summons you."

"We're not going on a mission for someone we've never laid eyes on."

"I understand. Lakom will show you out," she says casually as the three sisters get up from their thrones and start to leave the room.

"Wait!" Marcus leaps to his feet.

"Yes, Mr. Cane?" all three say at the same time.

"Are sure you can do what your father did and cast the Dy out?"

"Certainly."

Marcus addresses her with a steely coldness.

"If we get this Amulet thing and you can't fix my girl, I will destroy you, your city, and every damn thing in it."

"Agreed."

Chance has her sisters give us a tour around Adam City. We follow them towards the back of the temple and through a set of double doors. Adam City looks just like any bustling metropolis. The only difference is, everywhere you go, you see people using their powers.

Across the street from the temple, a lady disappears and reappears just in time to prevent her toddler from crossing the street on her own. A teenager uses his camouflage powers to leap out and scare his friends.

A block away, a man effortlessly lifts up his car and squeezes it into a parking space. In a grocery store nearby, a clerk does inventory by suspending fruits in the air and counting them. And a school of kids spill out into the schoolyard, making a game of throwing fire at each other and blocking it with their super-powered shields.

As the sisters walk through Adam City, they are met with smiling faces. But when the Quos see the team walking along the streets, they all stop and stare. Most of their attention is fixed on the Guardians' wings. Jay smiles at them but he gets nothing in return.

"They take time to warm up to winged ones," Choice explains.

"It's crazy to see how freely they use their powers here," Miku adds.

"It's hard to get over the 'no wings' thing," I tell the sisters.

"When you have great powers, you don't need wings," Choice replies with slight disdain in her voice. Marcus and I exchange a look. He caught her tone, too.

"My sister means to say, we're all gifted. Wings or no wings," Charity explains.

"Well, we know what Chance can do, what about you, Choice?" Rio asks.

A smile creeps onto Choice's face. She stops walking and goes over to Ameana.

She stands to the right side of Ameana and holds her hand out as if she is "calling" for something from inside Ameana's head. A few seconds later, a stream of long silvery thread seeps out from Ameana's temple and gathers in Choice's palm. Then Choice throws the thread against a tree. The tree turns into a pile of ashes instantly.

"Wow," I whisper under my breath.

"I collect thoughts. Anger. Hate. Fear. I take them and turn them into—"

"A weapon," Jay finishes.

"Something like that," she says coyly.

Jay stares back at her hard. I thought I would defuse the tension by focusing somewhere else.

"So Charity, what's your power?" I ask.

"Um…well, you can Glide, right?" she asks Jay shyly.

"I can Glide and Convince," he replies.

"How far can you Glide in a second?"

"About halfway around the world."

"Take my hand, then try to Glide."

She extends her hand and Jay takes it. A blue spark ignites between their hands, then Jay Glides. He comes back in a fraction of a second.

"Yo, that was crazy!" he announces.

"You went all the way around the world?" I ask.

"Six times," he says, too excited to stand still.

"I'm an Enhancer. I add to whatever powers you already have," she says dismissively.

"That's hot!" Jay says, clearly impressed.

Chapter Six: Adam City

"I wish I could have my own power and not just make other people stronger."

"Charity, don't be a downer," her sister scolds. She hunches her shoulders slightly and lowers her eyes.

"Charity, your power is like cash money. It's always useful," Jay says. She doesn't bring her eyes up from the floor all the way but she does perk up and smile.

"We need to go inside," Ameana says weakly as she doubles over in pain.

"What is it?" Marcus asks, rushing to her side.

"I don't know."

"Does your power have some kind of side effect on the people you pull from?" Marcus asks.

"It makes them weak. I should have mentioned that," Choice says sweetly.

"Yes, you should have," Marcus warns her.

Rio makes Ameana lean on him as we all head back to the temple.

As soon as we enter, Chance is there to greet us.

"What do you think of our city?"

"Nice. But if we are going to get to Pyron, we should head back now," Marcus informs her.

"It's late. The Port can only take you as far as Terra. And you should not travel there at night."

"We can take our chances," he assures her.

"Your teammate looks unwell; Recharge, then leave in the morning. We have prepared rooms for all of you."

Marcus is about to object but then he looks at Ameana. She is trying to put up a brave front but she has yet to stand fully upright.

"Okay, but we will take off at first light."

"That sounds very wise, Guardian."

Chance tells Charity to show us to our rooms.

"Before you go, I think it's only fair to warn you that Pyron will be extremely dangerous. Everyone always focuses on reaching Kairo but that's a mistake. You will need to focus on how to get past the terrain of Pyron first. Then focus on Kairo in the castle."

"You have any suggestions?" the twins ask.

"You will need help from three beings. You need someone very familiar with Hun's Market as Kairo has used many items from there to protect his land."

"Would a Seller do?" I reply.

"That would be wise, yes."

"Do you know of one?" Charity asks.

We all exchange bemused looks.

"Yeah, we know one," Marcus says regretfully.

"Is he a friend?"

Is Tony-Tone a friend?

"He's…well-meaning," I say out loud.

"He will be important to your mission," Charity says, concerned.

"Next you will need someone who knows Kairo and how he thinks."

"I know a guy who is obsessed with all things Kairo. He's studied him for many Cycles. He'd love to go with us."

"Good. Lastly, you will need a Para," Chance concludes.

"Why?" Ameana asks incredulously.

"You will be invaded by darkness from all sides. The light of a Para will help to combat the ubiquitous evil around you."

"Do you know a Para?" Choice asks.

We all look at each other and then at Ameana. She sighs softly and nods "yes."

"One final matter: we would appreciate it if you would not tell anyone about us until after your mission."

"You want us to keep all of this a secret, why?" Jay asks.

"We would like to personally introduce ourselves. That will give us a chance to make a good impression on the Angel world. If word gets out about us before we're ready, we can imagine the misgivings and rumors that will follow. So we feel secrecy is best. Do you agree, Marcus?"

He agrees to her condition.

"Then, by morning you and your team should be off. If you fail to recover the Amulet—"

"We. Won't. Fail," Marcus swears. Chance merely smiles and says that is her hope as well.

Chapter Six: Adam City

Charity shows us to our rooms. Marcus tells Jay to contact the guy he knows and orders us to get some rest. We are to meet back in his room in a few hours. We all follow instructions. I give Marcus a quick kiss and head to my room.

The minimalist décor makes the room an ideal place for meditation. I can't help but think how happy Wolf would be in here. I laugh to myself thinking what awful things Ameana would do to me if she knew I was even *thinking* about Wolf. Even if it is an innocent thought.

I look at myself in the circular mirror before me. There is a smile on my face. Outside of being with Marcus, I have found little reason to smile of late. Now I think there is actually a chance that I may be saved right along with the world. I never allowed myself to entertain such thoughts before. Now, I'm thinking about what college I may go to and where I will be in five years…

We're going after Lucy's son and it's been predicted that not all of us will make it back. Maybe you should hold off the long-term planning, Emmy.

Given this kind of thinking, I know if I stay in this room I will drive myself crazy with worry. So I head over to Marcus's room. The team is supposed to be Recharging but if I know my First Guardian, he's wide awake.

As I walk by Miku's room, I hear her and Ameana talking. I guess no one is Recharging.

"I know we're good and we've gone up against a lot. But Kairo?" Miku says.

"I know," Ameana says with a sense of dread.

"Kairo is a psychopath."

"Yeah, I agree. I'm not sure Lucy could kill him even if she wanted to."

"Going up against him is worse than Hun. Do you remember what he did to Linden?"

"I heard that story in training and it gave me nightmares."

Who's Linden?

The two fall silent.

"We don't really have a choice, do we?" Miku says a few moments later.

"No. Marcus is going to do this with or without us. And we can't let him do it alone."

"You guys think I'm crazy for not wanting to kill the Tics?" Miku asks.

"I get it. Redd hurt a lot of people. You're trying to undo some of what she did."

"Exactly. I put my hand through a man's chest and ripped his heart out from his body. And you know what is worse? How much I enjoyed it."

"That wasn't you."

"Redd is a part of me. So somewhere inside me I'm actually that dark and that twisted."

"I know it's difficult to look back on, but when you're in the heat of a battle, you can't take regret with you. It'll slow you down."

"I just can't believe how out of control I was. How could evil make a home so easily inside me?"

"It's not just you. Angel or not, it's easy to let evil in. Some days you keep it a bay and some days it comes up to your door and knocks."

"Have you ever…let it in?"

"Gotten very close."

"When Emmy kissed Marcus?" she asks carefully.

"Yeah…"

"At least you were strong enough not to do something crazy, unlike me."

"You don't know how many times I've separated Emmy's flesh from her bones in my head."

"Ameana!"

"What? I know it would be wrong but it would also be fun; so much fun." I can hear the smile in her voice.

"I thought angels were supposed to be nice?" Miku teases.

"No, Pretty. We're supposed to be good and I am. Have I killed the human? No. But thinking about it is fun. And we are allowed to have some fun."

"I guess. So, how do you feel?" Miku asks her.

"Much better, the side effects of Choice's powers are wearing off."

"I don't mean that. I mean the fact that we're about to ask for Wolf's help."

"Pretty, there has to be someone else we can ask."

"Wolf may not kill but you can't deny he can handle himself. Or as Jay would say, 'kid's got skillz,'" Miku says, imitating Jay's voice.

"I know but…"

"Ameana, it's okay to like him."

"What if I don't want to?"

"I hate what you're letting the breakup do to you," Miku says gently.

After a moment of reflection, Ameana admits, "Wolf is kind of sexy when he fights. And his wingspan is *massive…*" They share a sinful laugh between the two of them.

"Wait, we shouldn't judge an angel by his wingspan," Ameana says.

"Um…what else are we supposed to judge him by, his soul?" They share yet another laugh.

"Look at it this way, if Kairo kills us, we can die looking at the best set of wings this side of the light," Ameana adds.

"Mmmmm, now that's a good death!"

CHAPTER SEVEN: IT'S TIME...

I head to Marcus's room. I enter and find him standing by the window. His room is decorated very much like mine: simple "earthy" elegance.

"I think Miku is still hung up on what she did as Redd," I inform him.

"Yeah, I got the feeling when she basically suggested we play nice with Tics who were trying to kill us. I thought maybe she'd get around to talking to Ameana about it."

"She did. They're in Miku's room. Ameana is sharing her innermost fantasy about taking my life."

"Did you tell her to get in line behind Lucy and the Akons?" he says. I smile and lean in to kiss him. The sparks from his kiss always ignite something in me.

"Are you okay with her and Miku being so close?" he asks.

"They knew each other first. Anyway, she and I get to have our little ...talks."

"Really? About what?"

"Stuff," I say, blushing as I turn away.

"What did you two talk about?" he says, studying my face with growing interest.

"Unicorns, pillow fights, and nail polish."

"So you won't tell me?"

"Nope."

"I could persuade you," he says, pulling me closer.

He kisses the nape of my neck gently. I exhale softly and wisely pull away. If I let him, he would be able to get every embarrassing detail out of me. Actually if he continues to kiss me the way he is, I would act out my conversation with Miku in sock puppets. Marcus is wrong. His power isn't his strength or his ability to reflect a person's fear back to them. His real power is in his touch.

"Don't distract me, Guardian; I'm here on a mission," I say with my best "official" voice.

"What is your mission?"

"To get my hottie boyfriend to open up to me."

"Open up about what?"

"Kairo. How dangerous is he?"

"Emmy, don't worry. You know I'll protect you."

"Yeah, I know. But who's going to protect you and the rest of the team?"

"It's our job to put our lives in danger. You know that."

"I also know that the mission would be complete if you weren't in love with me."

"But I am."

"I need to know. How dangerous is Kairo?"

"All you need to know is that your angel loves you more than his own soul."

I am about to argue but there is a knock on the door. The rest of the team wanders in.

"I guess no one could Recharge, huh?" Marcus asks.

"Not after finding out all this craziness. Are we really taking on Kairo?" Rio asks.

"We don't have a choice," Marcus replies.

"I was taking a look around the temple and there's a room filled with beds. Like hospital beds," Jay says.

"What do they need it for?" I ask.

"I asked Charity and she just said it was for extra guests."

"So?" Miku says.

"So, who has fifty extra people sleeping over?" Jay asks.

"It could be nothing," Ameana says.

"That's just it, you guys. It *could* be anything. I think we're moving too fast on this. I know the council isn't perfect but why would they deny the existence of a whole race?"

"They did that because they were afraid of the balance shifting," Miku replies.

"I don't know. I'm not sure we should be undoing anything the council has done," Jay protests.

"We brought Rio back," Miku replies.

"That's different."

"No, it isn't. The council isn't perfect. They never should have denied the Quo the right to equality. Now we get to correct that," Marcus says.

"This has nothing to do with equality. You want to save the human," Ameana says.

"It's been almost a year now. Can you just say my name?" I ask, no longer hiding the irritation in my voice.

She ignores me and addresses the team.

"Jay does have a point. We need more time to dig deeper into the Quo."

"We don't have time. There is a price on Emmy's head. Every single evil entity is looking for her," Marcus replies.

"The council hid an entire race from us. I just think we really need to find out why," Jay insists.

"The Triplex is in Emmy. The council hid that from us, too. They do whatever they want," Miku reflects.

"I'm just saying we need to slow down," Jay adds.

"Again, we don't have time," Marcus objects.

"Look, man, I know you love Emmy. I love baby girl, too. But you are walking into a ridiculously dangerous situation without enough info," Jay warns.

"What do you want me to do? Google 'Quo People'?" Marcus snaps.

"Let's go back to the Sage, maybe he knows something."

"No. I'm not wasting any more time," Marcus vows.

"He's just telling you to be careful, Marcus. We could go to Pyron and it could be some kind of trap," I inform him.

"I get that, Emmy. But it doesn't matter. It's the only way to keep you alive."

"Were they being honest when they said they are the triplets from the story?" Miku asks her twin.

"Yes, but they do have secrets."

"That's everybody," Ameana says.

"When they talked about their history, was it true?" I ask.

"It's not that simple. The sisters are radiating a lot of things. But it could be because they are lying to us about something or because they have their own personal issues going on. For example, Charity is so hot for Jay she's about to jump out of her skin."

Normally Jay would use that opportunity to make a joke but he doesn't. He must really be worried about this mission.

"We need to talk to the Sage," Jay says again.

"No time," Marcus insists.

"Can we at least call him?" Ameana wonders.

"I tried calling, there's no cell service here," Jay replies.

"Jay, you've always had my back. What's changed?" Marcus accuses.

"I have always had your back, but you're compromised. I get it. You're in love. But if you're not thinking clearly, then it's our job to get you to stop and think about what you're doing," Jay pleads.

"I know what I'm doing."

"Is that why we lost Reese? Is that why we almost lost Rio?"

"I'm so sick of you throwing that in my face. How many times have I helped make a win happen for this team? How many Cycles is it going to take for you to forgive me for Reese's death?"

"He was my best friend. Every single day, he's on my mind."

"He's on my mind, too, Jay."

"That's crap. The only one on your mind is, and always will be, Emmy."

"What the hell do you want from me? Huh? You think hating me will bring Reese back?"

"I think forcing you to focus will prevent us from dying a tortuous death."

"Oh and when you came down here on this mission, was that your goal, Jayden? To make sure you had an easy death?"

"I wanted not to die at all."

"Then you never should have agreed to be a Guardian. We don't get to choose how we die. We get a mission and we complete it. Period."

"This isn't about the mission. This is about you going off and making the whole world pay because you fell in love."

"What?"

"You heard me, Marcus!"

"Okay. I'll tell you what, Jay. I'm gonna ask you and everyone in this room a question. If anyone raises their hand, then we can call this whole thing off. I will take Emmy's life right here, right now."

Everyone in the room stands still. My heart races and my palms go cold.

"If any of us raise our hand after you ask the question, you're gonna just let everything drop?"

"Yes."

"Fine. What's the question?"

"If anyone in this room thinks Emmy wouldn't risk her life to save them?"

The silence is so loud it practically buzzes. Marcus waits. No one raises their hand.

Marcus asks the question again. And again, no one raises their hand.

"Then explain this to me: how come the girl with no wings and no powers is willing to die for us but we're running like hell when it's time to save her?"

Marcus waits earnestly for a response. No one has anything to say. Marcus then confesses to the group softly:

"I know this is going to be beyond difficult. But I'm not asking my team to follow me into battle; I'm asking my family."

Jay is the first to respond.

"I got you. For real."

The others nod silently.

"Thank you," Marcus replies.

"Um…I don't want to ruin this 'all for one and one for all' moment, but who is Linden? And what did Kairo do to him?" I ask.

They all look at each other. Rio is the first to speak.

"Linden was a Traveler angel. He wasn't very good at it. He was always failing to report to the council because he'd get caught up with his true passion, painting. His paintings were so genius, he was commissioned by all of the Original Paras and basically every angel in the light."

"Kairo heard of Linden's work. He asked Linden to paint him. Linden refused. He said he would rather die than do it. Kairo was livid. He sent demons to capture Linden and bring him to the castle."

"He killed Linden?" I ask, unable to hold back.

"No," Miku says. "He cut off Linden's arms and legs. He then placed him in a dungeon with full sets of paints and brushes to taunt him. Kairo force-fed Linden a mixture to take away his short-term memory. So every day he wakes up thinking he can paint, then he witnesses the horror of his mutilated body. He screams and cries every time like it was the first time."

"Oh Omnis, why would he do that?" I beg.

"Kairo isn't turned on by pain alone. He likes to get inside your head and make you *wish* you were dead," Miku explains.

"It's been said if you stand still on a windy day and you hear the wind howling, that's Linden calling out 'Kill me, kill me' over and over again," Rio adds.

"He's sadistic," I say, mostly to myself.

"Lucy made him, so…yes, he is," Ameana concludes.

"This is the guy we're going after? Marcus, we can't. If he gets any of you, he'll torture you guys for eternity."

"Emmy, he won't get us," Marcus promises.

"Has anyone ever tried to find Linden?"

"No one has made it inside the castle."

"How many years has it been?" I ask.

"Not years. Cycles."

"Cycles?"

My heart sinks. I don't want to know any more about Kairo. I just want everything to be still. I want to somehow make this all go away. I sit down on the bed and shut my eyes. The picture of the mangled painter flashes in my head.

We can't go up against that kind of lunatic. How do you defeat a psychotic demon that the angels aren't allowed to kill?

I'm so deep inside my head I don't realize that the team has left Marcus and me in the room alone. He sits down next to me.

"Look at me," he asks gently.

I shake my head "no."

He reaches out and slowly turns my head to face him. A fresh stream of warm tears flows down my face.

"He's gonna torture you," I sob.

He pulls me into his chest. I sob against him. He strokes my hair and kisses my forehead.

We're quiet for several minutes. The only sound is my crying.

"I can't let you do it. I can't let you guys face Kairo."

"Hey, look at me," he says again.

I reluctantly look into my angel's face.

"Nothing Kairo does to me will ever compare to what your absence does to me."

"But, Marcus—"

"Emmy, the first few weeks I came to Earth and I tried to stay away from you, those were my days of torture."

"I can't handle you guys dying for me."

"It's an angel's honor to give up their lives for courageous humans."

"I'm not courageous. Courageous humans don't cry into their boyfriend's chest."

"They do. And then they dry their eyes and get ready to battle," he says as he dries my tears with tissues from the box by the bed.

"I'm not really worth all of this…"

"You are the most important thing in my life. But that doesn't matter if you think you're worthless. I can't give you any value. You have to give that to yourself."

"I don't know why all of this is happening. I'm just some girl."

"You had a mother who loved you. You have a father who would fight me to the death if it means protecting you. You also have a boyfriend who would lay down his life for an extra minute with you. How could so many people be wrong?"

"You don't ever doubt me, do you?"

"No. I've seen you in action. I've seen you in hell, and hell bowed down to you. So I know what you're capable of. Emmy, it's time you had a little faith in Emmy…"

CHAPTER EIGHT:
IF I DON'T RETURN

Once we're back in New York City, Jay has Marcus call up his buddy who has been studying Kairo. His friend suggests that if knowing Kairo's mindset is vital, he should seek out the number one Kairo historian: Isabelle Gonzales. We meet the angel at a small café near my house.

Isabella is a pretty Latina with dark brown eyes, rich curly hair, and glasses. Her slight accent makes her even more endearing. When she enters, she begins speaking in Spanish. Angels speak every language, so the group joins in.

"Hey, don't leave out the human who only got a C in Spanish."

"I was just telling the Guardians I can't believe how close I am to the map," she says, leaning in to study my eyes.

I smile and try not to feel weird about her being so close. I fail. This is totally weird. It's like being on display.

Please stop looking at me…

"Does it hurt?" Isabelle asks.

"Not really, no."

Please stop looking at me…

"When you blink, can you feel it move?"

"No."

Please stop looking at me…

"What happens when you wash your face?"

Why can't I be invisible just for a few minutes?

Rio and Marcus sense my discomfort because they rescue me.

"Isabelle, we heard you know 'all things Kairo.' Is that true?"

"No one here or in the light has done as much research as I have," she says proudly.

"And what have you learned?" I ask.

"Most demons have a desire to cause physical pain, but for Kairo that's only secondary. His first priority is anguish. He likes to make his victims die a thousand mental deaths before he actually kills them."

"So we've heard," I reply.

"I'm fascinated by Kairo; always have been. For example, did you know that while Lucy created him from a number of depraved mixtures from Hun's Market, she also added a human component?"

"And what was that?" Miku asks.

"No one knows. Lucy destroyed the Seller who gave it to her. All that's known is that somewhere inside that body of evil and malice there's one human element."

"Well, from what I've heard about him, it's not mercy," I inform Isabelle.

"That's the question posed by historians everywhere: What kind of human emotion does Kairo have? Can it be used to nurture a more humane, understanding version of him? Is he evil because he was created this way or because he chooses to be?"

"You sound like you admire this guy," Ameana says, put off by the thrill in Isabelle's voice.

"The more we know about evil, the easier it is to destroy it," she defends.

"How close have you gotten to destroying Kairo?" Rio inquires.

"Not close at all. I've read accounts of his terror but I've never seen it firsthand. I can't help but feel that if I was able to study him up close, I could get the info I need to know what he's really like."

"How do you feel about seeing him in person?" Marcus asks.

"Very funny."

"He's serious," I add.

"You guys are going to Pyron?"

"Yes. Kairo has something that belongs to some friends of ours. We need to get it back. You would be extremely helpful on this mission. If you need to think about it—"

"I'm in!"

"You understand this isn't a road trip to Las Vegas, right?" Miku asks.

"She knows and she's excited," Rio confirms.

"Look, Isabelle, reading about a demon and taking him on face-to-face is different," Marcus warns.

"I know it sounds crazy but I think I could really help you guys. I've been looking for this opportunity for many Cycles now. I can do this."

"We don't doubt that. But we want you to know about the danger you will face," I plead with her.

"I'm ready. I want to help."

"Are you sure?" I ask again.

"Yes. When do we leave?"

"Later tonight."

She smiles. Jay, who's been surprisingly quiet, asks a question.

"You're the first angel I've met that wears glasses," Jay says.

"I read a lot."

"Yeah, okay. But angels have perfect eyesight. I mean it's like a trillion times better than humans'. How many books could you read to actually require glasses?"

"A hundred thousand, give or take."

"Damn! So, what, you don't ever get to chill?"

"That's how I 'chill.' What could be more fun than a book?" she asks innocently.

Jay looks dumbfounded. I playfully jab him in his side. The rest of the team holds back laughter.

"Yo, I would love to show you what's more fun than reading," he says slyly.

"No thanks."

"Oh, you're seeing someone?"

"No."

"Then, what's the problem?" he pushes.

"Well, um…"

"You don't date Guardians? You think we're all players?"

"Honestly, just you," she says, looking around at everyone at the table. From that point on, the two go at it as if we aren't there.

"Yo, why you try'n to do me dirty? You don't even know me," Jay says, highly offended.

"I've read about you in the Splash."

"That mess is garbage."

"So you don't read it?" she asks.

"No. Well…I browse."

"Well, it's not just them. Everyone says you're the love 'em and leave 'em guy."

"Who says that?"

"The ones who've loved and left I guess. Look, I'm not trying to be mean or anything, it's just that I'm looking for…"

"For what?"

"A guy who's…ugly."

"What the hell does that mean?"

"I mean, you're a very handsome, attractive guy; too much so. You look like the centerfold for 'hot 'n' perfect.' Everyone knows, the hotter the angel, the bigger the jerk."

"True," Miku agrees. Her eyes widen. I don't think she meant to say that out loud. Jay glares at her and returns his attention to Isabelle.

"So you ain't feel'n the kid cuz he's fine?" Jay admonishes.

"I'm just saying I date guys who aren't so…polished; guys who haven't practiced smiling in the mirror."

"First, I don't need to practice; this is all natural. Second, maybe if you'd stop being so judgmental, you'd be able to do more than read about people's lives. Maybe you'd actually have one."

"I'm sorry if I'm not gushing all over you, Guardian. I know you're supposed to be the Justin Bieber of the Angel world but that just doesn't do it for me."

"Seems like you haven't 'gotten it' in a while."

"Is your ego so small that rejection from a stranger causes you to lash out like this?"

"What about your ego? You think you're a better angel than me just because you don't get around like I do?"

"Who says I don't?"

Chapter Eight: If I Don't Return

"Oh, I'm sure you and the other librarians get really crazy. I heard you guys have even been known to dog-ear the page!"

"Why don't you just go off and do like your kind usually do: flirt with some brainless girl who has to write directions to the light in the palm of her hand so she won't forget."

"I'd rather her be dumb than uptight. I mean for real, it would be easier to get Lucy into the light than to get you to loosen up."

"Look, I don't date guys like you. Nothing you say will get me to change my policy."

"Yo, I don't even want you no more!"

"That took five minutes. I'm guessing that's the longest you've ever been with a girl?"

"Say what you want but just so we're clear, I don't flirt with every girl."

"Ha! You've scoped out every chick in here, including the one on the poster."

"She's holding cake. I like cake."

"Yeah, I'm sure you do…"

"ARGH!" Jay barks.

Best. Argument. Ever.

Jay is absolutely livid. He stares back at Isabelle, who is fuming. The two stare at each other as if to kill the other. Then Isabelle leans back in her chair and smiles.

"So, you're saying you're not the kind of angel who flirts with everything that flies?"

"That's right."

"Care to prove it?"

"Hell yeah."

"You'll have to go the rest of the day and not flirt with anyone."

"You gonna follow me?"

"No, I have a friend who makes Truth Stones. It's a very basic version of Rio's powers. It looks for one emotion: desire. I have one here."

She takes out a small bracelet with black stones strung together.

"It's held by Samson string. So only my hand will be able to untie it from your wrist."

"This is gonna monitor how much I flirt?" Jay asks.

"Yes," Isabella says, just as she exchanges a quick glance with Rio. I look at Rio as if to ask what's going on. Rio suppresses a smile and shakes his head.

"We just met and you're already try'n to tie me down…" Jay says.

She places the string of black stones around his wrist.

"How does it work?"

"Every time you feel desire, one of the stones will turn blue. There are twelve stones in all. If we meet tonight and all the stones have turned blue, then I was right."

"Fine, but when we meet up and all the stones are still black, I want an apology so heartfelt, it would make Omnis weep."

"Fine, whatever," she says as she gets up and heads out the door.

"Can you believe that chick? How dare she act like I can't control myself?" Jay asks.

We all look away from him.

"What y'all try'n to say?"

"Nothing. It's just that you're very…friendly," I say gently.

"C'mon, baby girl, don't do me like that."

Before we left the diner, three of the stones had turned blue.

We ignore Jay's ranting about how the stones must be defective and head over to Tony-Tone's shop. As usual, he has on an obnoxious Hawaiian T-shirt and chain. He greets us with his arms wide open. No one on the team is eager to hug Tony-Tone, but I don't have the heart to leave him out there with his arms wide open. So I hug him back.

"Hi Tony," I say as he squeezes me tightly.

"You know, I gotta be honest, I didn't think you guys would remember," Tony says to us.

"Remember what?" Ameana asks.

"Ha, ha, very funny. Like you don't know today is the anniversary of my original death."

"Tony, we didn't know," Miku tells him.

"Oh. So you never got the evite?"

"Ah, no," Rio says.

"I guess that's what happens when I'm in your spam folder."

"Sorry," Miku says.

"Oh. And I'm guessing there's no gift?"

"No."

"I see," he says, trying to hide his face.

"We need to talk to you about our mission," Marcus says.

"Yeah, I'm sure you do, but I'm not interested. You need to go to another Seller."

"Why?" I ask.

"Why, human? Because Tony-Tone is tired of being pushed aside. I send you emails, I call, and I text. Nothing. It's like we're not even friends."

"We are your friends, Tony," I insist.

"Yeah, that's what I thought, too. That's why I set up all your Facebook accounts. You guys can fly around the world, take on Rage, take on Hun, but you can't respond to a friend request. Unbelievable."

"Look, Tony—" Marcus starts with a firm, no-nonsense voice. I signal for to him to remain calm. We need Tony to come with us. And yes, Marcus can force him, but it's much easier if Tony comes willingly. I think Marcus agrees because when he speaks next, his tone is much softer and controlled.

"We know that you've done a lot for us, Tony. We appreciate all of it."

"You should. I can't tell you how many demons have come to me looking for a way to kill Emmy."

"You didn't sell them anything, did you?" I ask.

"No, but they can just go somewhere else. You're in real danger this time, no lie."

"That's why we came to see you."

"We need you to go somewhere with us," Ameana says.

"Me? You guys really want me to come along?" Tony says, flattered.

"Yeah."

"It is far away?"

"Well—"

"It's okay if it is. I have a killer road trip playlist. It's got all the greatest. If it's an overnight though, I'll need to go home and get a few things. Let's see…my silk eye mask, sound machine, lavender face scrub…"

"We're going to Pyron," Marcus informs him.

"The only thing in Pyron is—"

"Kairo."

"You want me to go with you to see Kairo?"

"Yes."

"Just because I can die and come back doesn't mean I want to die again. What if this is it for me? What if I've done too many bad things and my Cycle runs out?"

"We're not trying to get you killed."

"You know that guy doesn't just kill. No. No way. I'm not going. I like my limbs."

"Tony, we really need you to do this for us," I say to him.

"Sorry, no. I can't do it," he insists.

I am about to protest when Marcus signals for me to let it go. The team heads for the door but Marcus makes sure before we go, Tony-Tone overhears him:

"It's better this way. We need a Seller who knows everything there is to know about items from Hun's Market. That's not Tony."

Rio catches on and joins in the conversation.

"You're right. We should ask that other Seller guy."

"Yeah, what was his name? Something with a D? Don? Dan?" Miku asks.

Tony-Tone interrupts us.

"Dale? That weeping oil salesman doesn't know anything. He's only come back to life twice. He's a newbie. You need a Seller who's died many times. A Seller who's at the top of his profession."

"We'll manage. And when we come back having fought Kairo, everyone will want to know the story. We'll give Dale all the credit. Dale can have his picture be on the front page of every Splash."

"Front page?" Tony asks.

"Yeah, he'll be making history. The first Seller to ever be part of an epic takedown."

I can practically hear the wheels turning in Tony's head.

"Look, I think I should go with you guys. I mean, I know how much the team depends on me," he says.

"You're the backbone of this whole mission, Tony," I assure him.

"I know. It's a hard role to play, but what are you gonna do?" Tony says, shaking his head.

"So, you'll go with us?" I ask.

"Yeah, why not?"

"Good, bring any items you think might help us get to the castle at Pyron," Marcus instructs. "I'll text you where to meet us."

"Okay, but when we get back, if we get back—"

"We'll friend you," we all vow in unison.

When we head out of the shop, Marcus tells Ameana it's time to call Wolf and ask for his help. Ameana is showing an emotion I'm not used to seeing from her: nervousness. She shifts her weight, tugs on her earlobe, and fixes up her already perfect hair. Marcus makes her put it on speaker in case Wolf has questions for the team.

"Hey, it's Ameana," she says awkwardly.

"Guess my karma's been good. Hey, Princess."

"Um…hi. I was wondering if you…well…we were wondering—"

"What is it?"

"I need your help. I know it's—"

"When?"

"What?"

"When do you need me?"

"Tonight."

"Done."

"Don't you want details?"

"You need my help. There's no other detail. See you soon."

Wolf ends the call. Ameana looks at us as if she's not sure what just happened.

"Um…I guess he's in," she says, trying to recover.

Marcus orders everyone to find a park or anywhere quiet and Recharge before it's time to meet up and take off for Pyron.

"Hey, I'm gonna go home," I tell him.

"I'm coming with you."

"You're afraid something will happen to me?"

"That's one reason. The other one is I don't want you to be alone when you say goodbye to your mom."

I look at him, puzzled.

"Emmy, ever since your mom's death, you never open her bedroom door. You've made it into a shrine for her. Since we're going somewhere filled with danger, yet again, you fear you may not return. So, you want to go home and say goodbye."

"You think I'm crazy."

"Crazy looks good on you."

He takes me home. I walk into the kitchen and the same memory floods my mind. Only a few weeks ago, I came in here and found my mom's heart had been ripped out by Lucy. I fight back tears and avoid the spot where her body lay. Marcus stands behind me and wraps his hand around my waist.

"You okay?" he whispers in my ear.

"Yeah, the kitchen is always…"

"I know. You ever think about moving?"

"No, I can't leave her."

"I know the feeling."

I turn to face him.

"What about you? Are you okay?"

"Yeah, I'm just grateful."

"For what?"

"I'm grateful the team is behind us. Grateful the Sage gave me the book of fairytales so I could read about Isis and Demetri. And I'm grateful you're in my arms. When we come back, we have to go put my Rah in the mountains."

"But I don't have a Rah to place alongside yours."

"It's okay, we'll put an item that really matters to you."

"Okay. The Sage, he said you had a question you wanted to ask me."

"Figures he'd bring it up."

"What is it?"

"I wanted to know if you ever felt…sorry that I entered your life."

"No."

"I mean—"

"I know what you mean. The answer is no. You asked me once before and the answer is the same."

"Just like that?"

"Just like that," I repeat, leaning in for a soft, sweet kiss.

Then Ms. Charlotte slides between our feet and meows loudly.

"I see you, girl. Give me one minute." She meows as if to say, "Hurry up!"

"Can you feed her? I need to go into…"

"Sure."

He takes Ms. Charlotte into the kitchen.

I walk up to my mom's room, take a deep breath, and open the door slowly.

It's exactly the way she left it. There's a book lying face down on her nightstand. Her robe is thrown carelessly across the bed—the result of being late for work. Her flowery scent lingers in the room. And in my mind, I hear her voice.

"Piglet, have you seen the TV remote? I swear, this time I didn't walk off with it…You found it where…in the freezer? Guess I did walk off with it!"

Then she would laugh. Her laugh had a melody to it. I look around the room as if she'll enter at any moment. She doesn't.

I sob loudly and sit down on her bed. I pull her robe up to my face. I smell her lilac soap in the fabric. I cry for a few moments and then make myself pull it together.

"Mom, I'm going away for a while. I will do everything I can to come back to you. But if I don't, I just want you to know that no girl ever had a better mom. You loved me and never once regretted having me. I will hold onto that with my dying breath. Thank you."

I can feel myself about to seriously break down now. So I head out the door to avoid falling completely apart. But before I go, I turn around and tell her one more thing.

"He loves *me*, Mom. He really *loves* me. Can you believe it?" I laugh. And she "laughs." Slowly I exit but decide to leave the door open.

"Were you laughing?" he asks.

"Yeah, it's…nothing," I say, shaking my head. I pick up Ms. Charlotte. We leave her with Ben and his mom. Before we go, I hug Ben extra tight. His mom looks on.

"Em, you're gonna see him in a few days when you get back from your uncle's," she says, laughing.

"Yeah, I know. I just can't get over how big he's gotten."

"Kids do that. When you have your own in a few years, you'll see what I mean."

Yeah, in a few years…

As we head out of my building I tell Marcus how surprised I am he didn't try to get me to stay behind.

"Has that ever worked?" he asks.

"Nope."

"Well, I'm learning."

Once outside, we find Isabelle, Tony-Tone, Wolf, and the team all waiting on us.

Jay looks disgruntled.

"What's wrong?" I ask him.

"He's all out of black stones," Isabelle volunteers. I cover my giggle with a fake cough.

Marcus brings us out of our jovial mood with a warning.

"The Sage has predicted that at least one of us won't make it back. So now is the time if any of you want to stay behind," Marcus offers.

Everyone looks at each other. Some are worried, some excited (Isabelle), but most of us are focused. Marcus takes that as a sign that everyone is ready and willing. He looks at me as if he needs to be assured. That almost never happens. I flash him my biggest smile.

"We're ready," I assure him. It works. When he speaks again, the First Guardian is confident and in charge.

"Pyron is just outside of Germany. It's not a long trip but with the wings, it can be tricky, so be careful. Rio, take Tony. I'll take Emmy. Let's go."

We take to the air and head to the place that, for at least one of us, will be our doom.

CHAPTER NINE: GOOD FOR THE SOUL

Marcus makes us land in a clearing a few miles into a forest. Once on the ground, I ask where we are and, as usual, "Wiki" Jay fills in the blanks.

"We're in the Black Forest in Southwest Germany. Pyron is up ahead."

"Seriously, how do you know this stuff?" I ask.

"Well, if you give people a chance, they might surprise you," he says pointedly at Isabelle. She rolls her eyes and looks away.

"We shouldn't fly into Pyron. We don't want Kairo to know we're here," Marcus says.

"Righteous," Wolf agrees.

As we begin walking along the path, Isabelle cautions us against touching anything. She warns that Kairo could have a number of traps laid out for unwanted guests.

The Black Forest is filled with dense trees, birds, and creepy crawling things that make me wish I wore a longer jacket. A few minutes later we come to the opening of an ominous looking path that leads up the hill. There's a message written on the ground in what I hope is animal blood.

"Leave Hope Here"

The team informs me that the message is written in universal text. That means it is written in the language that the viewer of the message was born speaking. So if I spoke German, the message would have appeared to me in German.

"I swear, you angels get all the great stuff: you get superpowers, speak every language, and you age like a minute every thousand years," I say, mostly to myself.

"Yeah, but we don't get cable," Miku counters with a smile.

"Is anyone else wondering about the message on the ground?" Tony asks nervously.

"Seems clear; we're doomed," Rio says, clearly teasing him.

"And this doesn't worry anyone?"

"Tony, dude, if you need to meditate, we can wait," Wolf offers.

"No we can't!" Ameana says in disbelief.

"Why won't you let him achieve inner peace?"

Ameana's jaw drops. She is too beside herself to talk. For the first time since I've known her, she is actually rendered speechless.

Jay whispers to Rio, "Yo, I know we're about to get killed by the son of all evil, but this right here, hilarious."

Rio can't help but smile at Wolf and Ameana, who are now both in need of calming meditation.

"Tony, nothing is going to happen to you," Marcus says.

Tony is about to reply when we walk into a patch of fog so dense it's impossible to see more than a foot ahead. I look back and the path has all but disappeared into the fog.

"Everyone stay close," Marcus orders as he surveys the area.

"From what I've read, once we get past this area, the castle should be up ahead," Isabelle offers.

"My illumination as a Para should be able to penetrate through this but it isn't. This fog isn't natural," Wolf says.

"Nothing here is," Miku adds.

I understand what she means. We're surrounded by trees, each one more menacing than the last. Some of the tree trunks resemble mangled human faces screaming in agony. A few of them have been split open to reveal a gaping maw. Some of them stand curved and twisted like an evil witch's gnarled fingers.

Pyron Field has been drained of all color. The landscape is a maze of morose grays and malevolent blacks. Dread, despair, and doom cling to every tree branch. The only thing alive and thriving is bloodcurdling fear and unrelenting sorrow. It's like Edgar Allen Poe and Sylvia Plath gave birth to a son and we're stuck inside his mind. "You know, it has a name," Isabelle offers.

"What has a name?" I ask.

"The castle. Everyone just calls it 'castle' but the actual name is Castle Relinque. It means 'abandon.'"

"Hey, I'm sure Kairo doesn't practice his smile in the mirror, he might be your type," Jay offers.

Isabelle never gets a chance to reply because all of a sudden, Tony's scream fills the air. We all turn and find him on the ground being squeezed to death by an enormous, translucent python.

"Stop moving!" Isabelle begs him. But the panic and horror in Tony's eyes tell me he's not going to take her advice. Sure enough, Tony wrestles even harder. Marcus goes to attack the snake.

"No! It's a Pity Snake. It feeds on confessions. If you attack it, it'll split itself in two and kill Tony faster."

Tony's screaming grows louder. The snake is more than half around him. He's no longer able to move the lower half of his body.

"Tony, he's looking for a deep, dark confession. You have to give it to him or he's going to kill you," Isabelle shouts.

Tony's eyes are tearing up. He's too scared to talk, let alone make a soul-crushing confession. He makes sounds and mumbles but doesn't form any actual words.

"Tony, say something!" Ameana pushes.

But Tony is held in the grip of fear and unable to talk. The snake inches higher. It squeezes Tony's chest and now has him completely immobile.

"If he doesn't confess, he's going to die," Isabelle tells us.

"I think I saw a Touch plant somewhere around here," Wolf says.

"That's perfect! Go find it and cut the liquid from its roots."

"How will that help?" I ask.

"The liquid from the root of the Touch plant is paralyzing. The snake will be immobilized for a few seconds. That's enough time to get Tony out."

"Ameana, go with Wolf to find the plant," Marcus orders.

The two of them take off quickly and disappear into the fog. I turn my attention back to Tony, whose face has now turned a ghoulish shade of blue. Blood seeps out of his nose as the snake coils itself around Tony's neck.

He's not going to survive…

"I cheated on a math test once," I shout over at him. Everyone looks back at me. I don't care. I won't let anyone else die. If I have to get Tony to fess up to save his life, then that's what I'll do.

"I met a guy online once. He asked for my pic and I was afraid he'd think I was ugly, so I sent him someone else's picture."

Then I saw it. Tony let a little bit of hope in. He parted his lips but he just couldn't get the words out. I pushed myself to give him one last confession; one that I was hoping to take to my grave.

"I planned to kill myself so I could be with my mom."

I can't bring myself to look at Marcus's face. I focus on the Seller. Tony chokes out five words that would ultimately save his life.

"I killed my best friend."

The words give life to a small mass of dark energy. It hovers in the air and the snake greedily swallows it. As soon as it does, it uncoils itself from Tony and slithers away. The team runs over to Tony, who is coughing and having a hard time controlling his breathing.

Wolf and Ameana come back just in time to see Tony being helped to his feet. He takes a bottle of water out from his knapsack and drinks. Everyone is watching him. He turns to us and for the first time ever, Tony isn't up for talking.

"Can we go now?" he asks harshly. Tony has never raised his voice to the team. Seeing him so uneasy and upset throws all of us off. Instead of moving, we all stand still, looking at him.

"WHAT?" he shouts.

No one says a word. He looks down at the ground, leans on a tree, and drinks from the bottled water once again. When he speaks, it's not the Tony we all know. His tone is reflective and filled with regret.

"Back when I was human, my best friend Anderson and I hung out together every day. We had been friends since we were kids. He was smart; book smart. He pushed me to try harder in school but I just wasn't gifted academically. No, my gift was talking people into things. I could sell sand to the desert.

"I owed some guys a few grand for some not-so-wise bets I had made. They weren't very understanding when I couldn't pay. They hired some lowlives to come to my apartment and 'take care of me.'

Chapter Nine: Good for the Soul

"Anderson had come down from school to see me. He knew where my spare key was hidden, so he let himself in. When the guys came, they thought he was me and they beat him to death. Crazy thing is, he didn't even want to come down that weekend. But my gift is talking people into things…"

There's more Tony wants to say. But judging from the tight grip he has on the water bottle, it would take a hundred Pity Snakes to get it out of him. Marcus goes over to Tony, places a hand on his shoulder, and says, "We need to keep moving."

Tony nods quickly and follows the team as they walk ahead. A few minutes later, he comes over to me and thanks me for helping him.

I smile and reassure him, "I do that for all my Facebook friends."

As we make our way through Pyron, the sounds that surround us get more and more threatening. The menacing gray skies give way to night and what was difficult to see in daylight is now impossible to make out.

"We need to stop, Marcus," Ameana says.

"No, we should keep going."

"We can't see anything."

"She's right. Even Wolf's Para powers are no match for this kind of night," Rio says.

"That's because it's a devil's night. That means it's a night made by Lucy herself. Well, at least that's what I read," Isabelle says.

"Thank you, Library," Jay snaps.

I whisper to Marcus that the team looks like they need to Recharge. He reluctantly agrees.

"We need to find a spot where we can hide. I don't want to think about what kind of creatures are lurking around here," he says.

"I can help you with shelter," Tony responds. He goes into his knapsack and takes out a small liquid vial.

"This black liquid is called a Cob. It's a pop-up hideaway. Just drip a few drops on the ground and a camouflaged cave springs up. It holds up to ten beings. This is one of my best sellers. Demons use it to hide from…well…you guys."

Tony drops a few drops on the ground and instantly a large cave pops ups. I am assured that just like the map in my eyes, the only reason I can see the tent is because I know it's there. We enter and are surprised to find how vast it is.

Tony tells us it can also block sound from reaching the outside. He says we can stay here for a few hours. But he warns us to be careful and remember that we can be seen once we leave the confines of the Cob.

"Us food-dependent beings have to stick together," Tony says, handing me a granola bar. Like humans, Sellers do in fact need to eat in order to live. I thank him and unwrap it.

Looking around the cave, I see everyone looks worried and tired. It then occurs to me that even with Wolf here, the angels are exposed to an unusual amount of darkness. It does make them weaker much faster.

A few feet away from me I can hear Jay swearing to Isabelle that he will do whatever it takes to find out how she "rigged" the Truth stones. She replies that he may need to join some kind of twelve-step program so he can gain control over his flirting "addiction."

Across the cave from Isabelle and Jay are Ameana and Wolf. I can't hear what he has said to her but she laughs. It was so spontaneous, it even surprised her. She looks up at him but breaks the connection abruptly. At the end of the cave, the twins look still and peaceful lying down on the floor Recharging.

It takes a few minutes but finally everyone in the cave is resting. Well, that is of course except for Marcus. Since I confessed to wanting to kill myself a few hours ago, Marcus has been trying to find every possible way to avoid talking to me.

"You okay?" I ask quietly.

"Fine. Sleep," he says in his First Guardian voice. I hate when he takes that tone with me. It means I've really pissed him off.

"You don't seem okay," I say gently.

"Well, I am," he snaps. He heads out of the Cob. I follow.

"What are you doing? Get back in there," he whispers, careful not to wake the others.

Chapter Nine: Good for the Soul

"I came because you're mad and I thought we should talk."

"Talk about what?"

"You know what."

"Oh, you mean about how you were planning on ending your life?"

"Yes."

"Why? It's no big deal. In fact, that sounds like a great idea."

"Don't be like that, Marcus."

"Tell me, how were you planning on doing it?"

"I don't want to do this with you."

"Tell me, how you were planning to do it?"

"What does it matter now? I changed my mind."

"The point is you were going to do it."

"Yes, okay? I was. My mother was brutally murdered in our own home. She was everything I had. So, yes, I was going to take my life. I'm sorry if I'm not as strong as Marcus Cane."

"You really don't understand what it is you have, do you?"

"What are you talking about?"

"You're alive. Do you know how many of us Guardians would give up our wings if it meant that we get to live again?"

"Look I—"

"How dare you even think about taking your life? What kind of heartless little girl are you?"

"I am not a little girl and you need to watch how you talk to me!"

"Oh, so I can't raise my voice to you but you can end your life?"

"I am not gonna do it anymore, so what's the problem?"

"The problem is you're selfish. You have everyone's love: the team, the Sage, Ben, your uncle, and me. And you were just going to leave us? You were going to leave *me?*"

His tone is so wounded it cuts through me. I lean in close and brush the side of his face with my fingers.

"I'm sorry."

"You have only one job as a human: hold on. That's it. When life gets terrifying, cruel, and unbearable, hold on. Death will come soon enough."

"I know."

"NO, Emmy. You don't know. I died. *I died.* And what no one tells you when you're human is this: so long as there is breath in your body, nothing is that bad. Nothing. You must remember that."

"Okay."

"Promise me."

"I promise."

Marcus pulls me in to kiss me but instead he throws me to the ground. Confused, I look up and see a massive fire spring up where I stood just moments ago.

The air is filled with Fire Swans. The only way to make them out is by the stream of fire they are hurling at us from above. Marcus calls on the team and everyone rushes out to us.

The Fire Swans take off furiously after us. We run through the woods as fast as we can. Jay manages to confuse some of them by Gliding in circles. But the rest can't seem to be distracted. They cut through the trees like skilled creatures of the sky. The sea of fire rages on behind us as we run for our lives.

No longer having a choice in the matter, the team takes to the air to battle the Fire Swans. Marcus grabs one by the neck. It furiously struggles against Marcus's hold. The Swan is able to break away and send an inferno of flames after Marcus. The blast hits Marcus in the face and he goes flying uncontrollably into the night sky.

Seeing that Marcus's end is near, the Fire Swan swoops down to finish the job. Wolf skillfully harnesses a white surge of power between his hands and hurls it at the Fire Swan. The Swan is able to dodge it in time, but Marcus uses that window to get up from the ground and take to the air.

The Fire Swan seems really angry about having lost its chance to kill Marcus. It takes to the air more determined than ever to kill its prey. But this time, Marcus is able to overpower the creature. The First Guardian pulls it apart. It cries out and then disappears in a ball of flames.

Meanwhile, a Fire Swan narrowly misses deep frying Isabelle. Jay spots her and tackles the swan out to get her. Ameana comes to their rescue as more and more Swans invade the area. The twins coordinate an attack by luring one of the Swans away and having Wolf blitz it from behind.

Many of the morbid trees are now engulfed in flames. I try to run to safety but before I can move, I hear the massive tree beside me giving way. I know it's gonna come straight down on me. I squeeze my eyes shut like a two-year-old wishing away monsters from under the bed.

But there's no heat rising from my flesh. There's no sound of bones breaking under massive weight. I look up and there he is, securing me in his arms as we soar into the sky. I exhale, nearly dizzy from relief.

"Cutting it kind of close, First Guardian."

"I had time." He smiles and sets me down away from the battle.

My relief is short-lived as I realize that Tony is nowhere around. I call out his name over and over again. Out of the corner of my eye, I spot him being dragged off by one of the Fire Swans.

I look around for something to hit the Swan with but I find nothing. Then I spot the knapsack that Tony brought with him. I run over to it but I don't know what any of the vials are for. I'm worried I could end up doing more harm than good by using them.

Then I find the plant that Isabelle said was a paralyzing agent at the bottom of the knapsack. I grab the rock with the sharpest edge, pound the plant until the liquid seeps out, and dig it into the Swan's wings before he can take to the air again.

He drops Tony and turns to me. The bird lashes out and hurls a lake of fire at me. Thankfully the liquid from the plant takes effect immediately; the Fire Swan is paralyzed mid-fire.

I go over and check on Tony. He tells me he's okay. When I look back, all the Fire Swans are either dead or fleeing. Exhausted, I lie down on the ground and try and catch my breath.

"Fire Swans don't come into the Pyron. They normally live in the castle," Isabelle informs us.

"What does that mean?" Tony asks.

"It means Kairo knows we're here."

CHAPTER TEN: INTO THE WOODS

Off in the distance we can make out the castle overhead. But Isabelle tells us that it's still at least half a day away. The team discusses taking to the sky since Kairo already knows we are here, but they decide to stay on the ground since it provides more cover. This news doesn't sit well with Marcus. He asks if there is a faster route. She tells him no matter what, this is the only path to get to Kairo.

Just before night falls once again, I decide to take a walk. Actually Marcus insists I stay no more than two yards away, so it not really a walk. It's more like take a step outside, then hear him scold me for taking that step.

As I head back from my "long stroll" I notice the most bizarre flower blooming between the cracks of a rock. This amazes me because it's the first pretty thing I've encountered since we came to Pyron. It's a flower with black and white polka dot petals. I pluck it out of the ground and inhale its scent; it smells like orange blossoms with a hint of spice.

Finding the only thing of beauty in this awful place makes me smile. And suddenly it occurs to me to try and make the best of this situation. After all, I'm with my boyfriend, I'm still alive, and sooner or later, Marcus and I will be together. Yes, there will actually come a time somewhere in the week and a half that we have left, where I will be alone with this hottie and no one will stop that from happening.

As I near the cave, I find Jay and Isabelle on guard duty. I think the two of them would make a great couple. Finally, Jay's met a girl who calls him on his issues. Jay's such a sweet guy and Isabelle is awesome. More importantly, Jay needs someone who won't be putty in his hands, like I am when he calls me "baby girl."

Chapter Ten: Into the Woods

"I never got the chance to say thank you for…ya know," I hear Isabelle confess.

"Thank me for what?" Jay asks.

"For saving me from the Fire Swan. That was…maybe you're not too bad."

"Wow, you suck at apologies."

"You're not making it easy."

"Why should I? You've been judging me since we met."

"You saw my glasses and thought I was a prude."

"Um…you are."

"No, I'm not."

"What's the craziest thing you've ever done?"

"You mean beside this?"

"This doesn't count."

"I broke my ex-boyfriend out of Bliss."

"You dated an ex-con!"

"Yeah."

"And you broke him out?"

"Yes."

"Hell, nah. I'm gonna need more."

"All angels aren't good guys. I didn't know that at the time."

"What happened?"

"He injured a human. He swears it was by mistake. Anyway, the council felt he would be better off going to Bliss for a few months. I read up on Bliss and found passageways in from the floor plans and I helped him escape. The council found out, sent the guy back to Bliss, and they Grounded me to Earth for six months."

"You were lucky. It could have been much worse. What happened to the guy?"

"He got out a few months later and dumped me. Said he wanted someone more…angel-like."

"What the hell does that mean?"

"He went after some Para chick. She had an amazing inner glow, never read a book in her life, and had a free love policy."

"Oh."

"I don't get it. You guys are angels; how come all of you are jerks?" she asks sincerely.

"As angels, we are capable of an extraordinary amount of love and charity. But we don't always reach our potential."

"Tell me about it."

"Did you love him?"

"I was starting to."

"Look, I came at you wrong back at the diner. I should have been more…ya know."

"It's okay. I still would have turned you down." She smiles playfully. He smiles back at her.

"Can you take this stone thing off my wrist please, it's turning green," he complains.

"Haha, funny."

"No, I mean it. All the stones are green now," Jay says, holding out his hand.

"That can't be," she exclaims as she studies it.

"Why? What does that—"

She leaps up from the massive stone she was sitting on and kisses Jay. At first he pulls his hand away as if to say "I'm not doing anything but kissing back." Soon though, his hands are through her hair and down her lower back.

Like Jay, I'm shocked. I cover my mouth with my hand to hide my goofy smiles. She just stood up and kissed him. It reminds me of when Marcus and I were in the car and I kissed him. It caused a lot of drama. I mean a lot. But honestly, I would do it again a thousand times just to feel his lips on mine.

Okay, Emmy. Let's put that thought in the "things to never say in front of Ameana" box and close it up.

"What just happened?" Jay asks, baffled.

"I lied before. The Truth Stone picks up two emotions. Desire and regret. In order for all the Truth Stones to turn to green, it means you regretted every desire you had since you put it on."

"You lied to me?"

"Yeah, I just never thought it would turn green."

"It's cool. Just keep doing what you did before."

"You mean this." She reaches over and kisses him again. Her hair is now illuminated. I love when angels get a hicky. It still trips me out that it reflects in their hair. She pulls away. He comes in for yet another kiss.

"Hey, you don't have a thing for Paras, do you?" Isabelle asked.

"No, but I got a soft spot for lawbreakers." Her laughter fills the air. I clear my throat before they can start kissing again.

"Oh, hey, Emmy," Jay says awkwardly.

"Hi," I say, sounding very much like a bratty little sister who caught her brother making out with his girl.

"Um…I'm, we were just, um…"

"Hey, is it me, or is it really bright out here? Some of us are absolutely glowing," I tease. Jay takes off after me and chases me around.

Suddenly we hear Rio a few yards away.

"We're saving the world here, guys, you might want to lower the purple Wave count!"

The growl sounds as if it came from hell itself. I look up to the ceiling of the cave. I tell myself it's in my head. Then I look around and every single being in the cave is on high alert. There's a silence in the air and it's pregnant with fear.

We wait.

"It's a Cray," Ameana whispers, a slight tremble in her voice.

Ameana's trembling? This is so not good.

"What's a Cray?" I whisper.

"It's just one," Marcus says hopefully.

"No, there's a cluster out there and they're coming," Tony replies.

"Every growl accounts for a Cray. So far, there's only one out there," Miku says.

"What's a Cray?" I ask again.

"We should move," Wolf says.

"If they aren't on to us now, they will be once we start running. The best thing to do is stay still. Like Marcus said," Jay says.

"All of us put together should be able to handle a Cray," Isabelle says, mostly trying to convince herself.

"Damn it, guys, what the hell is a Cray?" I ask, not for the first time.

"A beast that lives to hunt and feed. It's Lucy's oldest creation. It can't be killed," Rio explains.

"Does it want confessions like the Pity Snake?"

"No," Miku says regretfully.

"Then what does it want?"

"Flesh."

I really, really need to remember to stop asking questions…

"They can't see us," Tony says.

"No, but they can smell us."

Another growl makes its way into the night sky.

"That's two," Rio reports.

Suddenly the single growls give way to a chorus.

"It's a cluster, we gotta move!" Marcus orders.

Everyone darts out of the cave and heads outside. The team tries to take to the air but a swarm of Fire Swans hovering above make it impossible to take off. Marcus instructs us to head towards the castle. He grabs my hand and we take off at top speed into the thick of the forest.

It is then that I get my first look at the Cray. They're so horrifying they stop me dead in my tracks. I tell myself that I can't just stand here and wait for the beasts to attack me. I tell myself this is stupid and I need to run. But no part of my body listens to me.

The Cray towers over me. It looks like an enraged bull crossbred with a demon. The blood from his last meal drips from his fangs and down on to his blue-black skin. There's some kind of leftover body part sliding down his long claws. I look harder and make out teeth and what was once an eyeball.

Dear Omnis…

The Cray growls loudly and bares all his fangs. I'm shaking before the beast. All efforts to move are in vain. I stand there frozen before him. In a few seconds it will be my eyeballs sliding down his claws, my teeth.

Dear Omnis…

Chapter Ten: Into the Woods

I've seen this in movies before. I would yell at the screen and tell the stupid girl to run. What I didn't know at the time was that the girl in the movie is telling her body to run but the body has a mind of its own.

"EMMY, MOVE!!!" I hear Marcus but I can't get my body to comply. The Cray cuts through the air with his claws. I see them coming toward me but there is some kind of disconnect between my brain and my muscles. I can't even close my eyes because like the rest of me, my eyelids are frozen.

Run, stupid girl, run…

Marcus swoops in just in time to push me out of the way but not in time to save himself. The Cray knocks him down to the ground and strikes him with his claws. I watch in horror as four long, deep gashes form across Marcus's chest. A silver substance quickly springs from the wound.

My angel is bleeding…

"Marcus!" I shout.

"I'm fine, go!" he shouts.

I don't move until I see that he's well enough to get up from the ground. Then and only then do I take off. I want to stop and help when I see Jay trying to fend off two Crays.

"Emmy, go!" Jay says, as if he could read my mind. I force myself to take off further into the woods. I'm so far in now that I can't hear the battle raging on behind me. The entire forest is on mute.

I creep through the forest scared to death that I'm not alone. Something moves to the right of me. I turn quickly but don't see anything. Something moves to the left of me. I turn and again there is nothing there.

I hear something crack beneath me. I look down—it's only a branch. Relief washes over me. I remind myself to breathe. Before I can make it to the next tree I see them—three Crays marching straight for me.

They sniff the air and with a series of grunts they seem to agree that I'm nearby. I quickly pull back before they can spot me. There's a small opening under a bed of earth. It's only a few yards away. It's big enough for me to fit into but too small for them to follow me.

Can I make it to the opening before they spot me?

I lean against the tree and listen for their footsteps. I don't hear anything. If I'm going to try for the opening, now is the time. I decide to make a break for it on the count of three.

One…
My heart beats so fast, it's painful.
Two…
I'm holding on to the trunk of the tree so hard my palms are bleeding.
Three…

I leap out from behind the tree and run towards the opening. I'm two feet away when a Cray blocks the opening at the last second. I turn around and head back the way I came. They take after me. I run frantically through the woods. My body is making up for having frozen on me earlier. It moves with speed I didn't think I was capable of.

The forest goes by me in a blur. Every gust of wind seems to whisper "death is near." I run faster. The uneven ground makes it hard to navigate and the branches mercilessly cut into my skin. More than once I nearly fall, but each time I gain my balance and forge ahead.

I will not die here…

I'm so concerned about the beasts on the ground, I forget about the ones in the air. A Fire Swan sprays me with flames from above. I move out of the way, narrowly avoiding the bird's wrath. But in the process, I lose my balance and hit the ground, hard.

I'm knocked out for what I think was only a few moments. When I wake up, I'm bruised and aching all over. I open my eyes and look up from the ground. There is a cluster of Cray looking down hungrily at me. There's nowhere to run. Even if there was somewhere to run, my ankle is broken. I can't walk, let alone run.

They growl amongst each other for a few seconds and come to some kind of decision. I pray to Omnis they decide they're not hungry, but that isn't the conclusion that they come to. They decide the biggest of them gets first stab—literally.

The Cray plunges his claw into my flesh. I let out a bone-chilling cry that's unrecognizable to me. Blood gushes out of my legs like a dam that's just been broken. The other Crays lean in to help themselves. Just as I am about to pass out from the pain, I see a bright light from the corner of my eye…

The next time I open my eyes, I'm in a cave. Everything is blurry and spinning. A voice tells me to rest. I think it's Marcus but I can't be sure. The darkness pulls me under again. I'm not sure how long I've been knocked out but when I wake again, the first person I see is Marcus. Concern and guilt are etched on his stunning face.

"Stop," I whisper softly to him.

"Stop what?"

"Feeling guilty." I try to smile but my face hurts.

"How are you feeling?"

"Like a lucky girl."

"How's that?"

"Did you see how fast I ran? I may have a chance at the next Olympics."

"The adrenaline kicked in."

"Whatever, next year I'm gonna try out."

He looks back at me. He's got this look on his face. It's not his serious First Guardian face. It's something else. I study him for a moment and then I understand, it's his concerned boyfriend look. Sexy.

"Marcus, I'm fine," I assure him. He helps me sit up and fills me in on what happened after the Cray stabbed me.

Wolf was able to distract them with a Powerball while Marcus rushed me to safety. Marcus left me with Tony. Then he joined the team and they were able to fend off the Cray.

I look down at my right leg. Someone has bandaged it and fixed my ankle. Marcus tells me it was Tony who was able to heal me with Woe. I remember the side effects of Woe from when Jay got hurt. Fortunately, it doesn't have the same effect on humans.

"So, I didn't walk around telling anyone I loved them?"

"No, it worked fine on you," Tony replies.

I ask Marcus about his wounds and he promises it's all been healed thanks to the Woe. Looking around the cave, I see everyone is fine. But there are two angels I don't see.

"Where's Wolf and Ameana?" I ask.

"Four Crays ganged up on Wolf. He's hurt."

"How bad?"

"Bad. Tony set up a Cob just for him so he can rest. Ameana is in there now, trying to convince him to leave the mission and go get help."

"He has to agree to go."

"Ameana's been trying but so far no luck," Rio says.

I stand up and head outside. Marcus warns me that I am not all better and that I should rest. I don't have time to convince him I'm okay. I have to see how bad things are with Wolf. Although the Woe worked on me, I still feel sore and ache just about everywhere. It takes me twice as long as I thought to get to the next cave.

I enter and find Wolf on the floor with half of his left wing torn off. There's a chunk of his torso missing. The only thing preventing him from bleeding out is the bandage at his side. The light in his perfect face has dimmed significantly. At this rate if he doesn't get help, he'll die.

For once, Ameana and I are on the same page. She looks up at me with profound sadness. Wolf looks stubborn and unwilling to listen to whatever it is she has been saying to him. He greets me with a small voice.

"You're really a centered human to survive the Cray. I would love to feel your aura sometime."

"Um…sure," I say, not really understanding what his request would entail.

"Wolf, you have to go back. Isabelle or one of the twins will go with you," Ameana says.

"I gave the team my word. Do you know what happens when you go back on your word? Ever hear of karma?"

"You ever hear of an angel surviving injuries like yours without going to Daraquin to get treated?"

"I'm not going."

"Why are you so damn stubborn?" Ameana shouts, about to lose it completely.

"She's right. You need to get help," I insist.

"I'll send the guys for some herbs and healing crystals. There's got to be some around here."

"What about Woe, won't that help?" I ask.

"His wounds are too severe for Woe to have any effect," Ameana replies.

In the short time that I've been in the cave with them, even more light has dimmed from Wolf's face. As Ameana tries to convince him to go back, I glimpse a familiar expression on the Para's face. It's a look that I saw just a moment ago on Marcus.

Wolf isn't worried about the mission. He's worried about who he's leaving behind…

"Hey, can I see you for a second?" I ask Ameana. She reluctantly leaves Wolf and follows me outside.

"What is it?" she demands.

"Wolf is never gonna agree to go home and leave you here."

"Why? I can take care of myself."

"Yeah, I get that. But he's…Wolf. He's always trying to do the right thing. And leaving the girl he…he's not going if you're staying."

"You think I should offer to go back with him?"

"It's worth a shot."

"The team needs my help. They can't handle Kairo when they're two angels down."

"We'll be fine. Once you get to Daraquin, you can always come back. We can't let anything happen to Wolf, or any of you."

She says she needs to run it by Marcus. We head back into the Cob that holds the rest of the team. They discuss it and agree that Ameana should take Wolf back and stay with him. When Ameana tells Wolf she's going to accompany him home, he tries to hide his smile but everyone sees it. He has it bad for Ameana. Once Ameana sees how pleased Wolf is by the news, she suppresses a smile by focusing on fixing his bandage. Although there was nothing wrong with it.

I swear somewhere behind that wall of perfection and coldness, a girl is falling in love…

CHAPTER ELEVEN: TIME WITH YOU

After Ameana and Wolf head back home, I tell Marcus that while I'm not a hundred percent yet, I'm well enough for us to keep going. He takes me to the top of the cliff across from the castle. I hate to admit it but it looks intriguing.

Castle Relinque looks as though it was carved out of the mountain it sits on. It's built from some sort of smooth, glossy black stone. It reminds me of something out of a gothic romance novel. It would be a wonderful place to spend the night; well, that is, if a deranged lunatic didn't live there.

Although Kairo is the ultimate problem, the immediate issue is the vast lake that separates the castle from the cliff we're on.

"I'm a pretty good swimmer, if that's what you're worried about," I tell Marcus.

"Look at the water carefully."

There's a light reddish hue to the lake, I observe.

"That's because he's making a stew," Marcus says bitterly.

"What does that mean?"

"It's just a morbid joke. Angels call this type of lake a Stew Lake. It's what we call a body of water with a Vsk at the bottom. And before you ask, a Vsk is a device that takes anything solid and mangles it into chunks. The council has used it in the past to keep anyone from getting to them."

"That's why the water's a weird reddish color?"

"Yes. It's a mix of the red from human blood and silver from ours."

"How do we get around it?"

"We don't."

"We could fly overhead."

"I thought about that. When we were being chased by the Fire Swans, many would fly ahead of us in an attempt to surround us. But as soon as they got here, they'd turn back."

"There's some kind of force field or something?"

"That's my guess."

"Well, there has to be another way around it."

"We've watched the Swans. None of them have ever flown past this point. We'll have to turn around and find a side entrance."

"But Isabelle said there wasn't one," I protest.

"There may be one she doesn't know about."

"That's gonna take some time."

"A day or two at least," he says, filled with despair.

"Hey, I was thinking about it and maybe if I die, it wouldn't be that bad. I mean I would get to go to the bridge and choose the light," I offer.

"It doesn't work like that. If you die as a direct result of the mission, you won't go into the light. You won't go to the bridge, you'll go straight to limbo. Do you get that? Anything having to do with the mission goes into limbo if it's killed during that time."

"Oh, I didn't know that."

I look down onto the raging liquid death trap below. Marcus and I stay silent for a few minutes. Then I break it because I know it's time.

"Marcus—" I begin.

"Please don't, Emmy."

"Don't what?"

"Don't tell me some crap about how I have to consider letting you go. For the last time, that's not gonna happen," he snaps.

I don't say anything. If I open my mouth, we'll just get into some stupid argument and that's the last thing I want to do right now.

However, I think my boyfriend was expecting me to reply. The fact that I choose to remain silent throws him off.

"Sorry," he says, once he realizes the effect his tone had on me.

"It's alright, but we need to talk," I plead with him.

"Fine, but not about your death."

"It's okay because I don't want to talk to my boyfriend about my death either. I want to talk to the First Guardian."

"What does that mean?"

"It means I need you to think like the courageous leader you are and not the guy I've come to love. Can you do that?"

I take his silence as a sign that I should forge ahead with the conversation.

"Marcus, after Sara died and I retreated from the world, you brought me back. You told me that I couldn't try and save the world. It was too big a notion to wrap my head around. You said I should focus on the people I know and love. Do you remember?"

"Yeah, I do," he says quietly.

"That's what I need you to do. I need you to focus on this." I pull out a Spiderman action figure the size of my finger.

"What is that?" he asks.

"I was having nightmares once I went back to my apartment. Ben's mom said she could feel how sad and alone I felt. She said Ben could feel it, too. One night when I was babysitting him, he gave this to me. He has a ton of Spiderman stuff but this is his favorite. I asked why he would give it away and he said because I needed a hero.

"He was right. I do need one. I need a hero to make sure a kid like Ben gets to have a future. I need someone to focus on his perfect little face and protect him from evil. I know you love me. That's been my saving grace. But Ben is my heart. Be my hero; save him…"

He sighs heavily and nods, but he can't bring himself to look at me.

"I need to hear you say it. I need to hear you say that if we run out of time, you'll take my life and save the world."

"Okay."

"Promise me."

"Okay."

"MARCUS, SAY THE WORDS!"

"I promise. I will take your life…"

At first I think he's just saying what I want to hear. I think about getting Rio so I can tell if he's really telling the truth, but then he turns to me and I see it right there in his eyes: Marcus Cane is now making decisions as a leader.

He is no longer my guy protecting the girl he loves. He is now the First Guardian. I believe if the time comes, Marcus Cane will kill me.

Marcus pulls]   vo can try and figure out another way to get into the castle. I swear that girl has read every book ever written in the history of angel-kind. She references books written by other angels and tries to figure a possible entrance they may have missed. I watch as the two of them collaborate. It turns out I'm not the only one watching them.

"Hi, Jay."

"Hey, baby girl."

"I like her. She is perfect for you."

"We just met and you're trying to make me give my Rah away."

"You should."

"She is kind of cool."

"She lights up when you walk in the room."

"That's because she found someone she could argue with."

"She seems really special. What would be so bad about the two of you getting together?"

"Girls and missions don't go well together."

"She can handle herself. You won't have to save her every few seconds like Marcus has to do with me."

"C'mon, baby girl, you've saved him a few times."

"I just buy him a few seconds here and there."

"Well whatever you did, you got him hooked."

"Jay, how does the team feel about Marcus? Are you guys mad because we fell in love?"

"Mad or not, it's done."

"Yeah, I guess."

"I kind of get Marcus a little more now."

"How's that?"

"When we were battling and I saw the Swan go after Isabelle…"

"Awwwwww… My favorite Guardian is falling in love!" I playfully tease him.

"Hey, slow down, okay. I haven't even introduced her to Siren."

"Your car?"

"Hey, that car and I go way back. If she doesn't like Isabelle…I'm not sure what kind of future we have."

I laugh at him and whisper softly in his ear.

"Take it from me, Jay, don't fight it."

Just then Rio enters the room and tells us Ameana has texted him. She and Wolf arrived safely in Daraquin. Wolf is on the mend, although the injuries were extensive and will take time to heal.

"Can I ask you something?" Jay says to me.

"Sure."

"How long do you think one being can be committed to another?"

I turn toward Marcus, who is in the corner diligently plotting a strategy to enter the castle.

"Hopefully forever."

It takes nearly five hours but finally Marcus and Isabelle come up with a possible way ɔ let the team Recharge before we head out. Miku stands guard just outside the cave.

I am about to drift off to sleep when I hear someone call my name. Looking around, everyone in the cave is lying still on the ground. I lay my head back down and assume it was all in my imagination. Then I hear it again. I think it might be Miku. I get up and walk towards her.

"Emmy, over here," the voice whispers.

I look off to the side, a few yards away from Miku, and there's a being standing in the midst of the forest. It calls out my name yet again. I try hard to make out who it is but it's too dark. The being is tall and wearing light clothing, but for the life of me, I can't see its face.

The being signals for me to come over. Normally, I wouldn't, it could be a demon. But there is something *very* familiar about the figure. I slowly walk towards it. When I get close enough to make out who it is, I'm too shocked to do anything other than stare.

"Reese?"

The angel beams at me. I look him over from head to toe and it's actually him. He's wearing light casual clothing that makes him look like a perfect J Crew model. His easy smile and warm eyes look back at me. I rush to him and he holds me tightly. Tears fill my eyes. He pulls me away and says he's missed me.

"Wait…what are you doing here?"

"I think what you mean to say is 'Wow, Reese, you're more handsome than I remember.'"

"Wait, you're dead…"

"Rio was dead. He got another chance. Why shouldn't I?"

"They told me there was no way you could come back."

"Well, they lied to you. I'm here and I've missed you so much," he says, embracing me again.

"I'm not dreaming?" I ask.

"I could pinch you? You know I would enjoy that," he jokes.

"How is it you're alive?"

"I had something to live for—you."

"So, Lucy just let you go?"

"Let's not talk about it. Let's just focus on us."

"Wait, don't you want to talk to the team?" I ask.

"I can do that later. Right now, I just want to be with you."

"Wait, Reese, there's a lot I have to tell you. A lot has happened while you were …gone."

"You mean like you and Marcus becoming a hot item? I heard."

"I'm sorry, I really am. I didn't even know you liked me until—"

"Yeah, I know."

"I never meant to hurt you. I love you. I mean, like a friend."

"A friend? Wow, you really know how to hurt an angel, don't you?"

"That's not what I'm trying to do. The whole time you were gone, I've thought about what I would say to you if I ever saw you again. And now you're here and I'm screwing this up."

"Relax, Em, you're doing just fine. I know you love Marcus. I get that. I still can't seem to get over you though."

"How can I help? What can I do?"

"Well, in the morning we'll all be back to team stuff but I was hoping you would give me one night."

"One night to what?"

"Convince you that you belong with me."

"If Marcus and I weren't…I'm sure I would fall for you. Hard."

"But you're in love with Marcus and there is no changing that," Reese concludes.

"I'm sorry. I keep looking back to find the moment when I led you on."

"You didn't lead me on. You're the sweetest girl I've ever met. You have a soul most angels can only dream of."

"It's just like you to compliment me when I'm standing here telling you I love someone else."

"Well, Marcus has had you for almost a year now. I think it's only fair that I get one night with you; as friends."

"What do you mean?"

"Hang out with me for a few hours. I've come a long way to be with you," he pleads.

"What about the team?"

"We'll surprise them in the morning. But for now, I really would love to just spend some time with you."

He takes my hand and Blinks me to the edge of a small fishing pond. There are trees and bushes all around us. Unlike in Pyron, these trees are serene and tranquil.

"This is the place you and your family used to go fishing in, back when you were human."

"I'm flattered you remember."

"Of course I do. You used to drink river water and disappear into this memory."

"As often as I could. Now I get to share it with you."

He takes his sneakers off and starts walking into the lake.

"It feels so good; Emmy, you gotta get in here."

I shake my head and start to head back.

"Reese, we have to go back. We're on a mission. We have to—"

"Don't do this to me, please. This is the only moment I get with you. Then it'll be morning and you'll be his again…"

The desperation in his voice breaks my heart. I remember him in my room telling me he's been wanting to kiss me for a long time. I recall him telling me, how when he was human, he stood in his room earnestly learning lines from a poem for a girl who was never going to return his love.

My Reese is back…

"Just five minutes. That's all I want. Will you give me that?" he asks.

I'm so relieved that Reese is back in our lives, how can I deny him a few minutes? He looks so happy standing in the water.

I can put the mission aside for a few minutes, right?

I run full speed ahead towards Reese. As soon as I reach him, he tells me to let go.

"What?"

"Emmy, let go," he repeats.

Confused, I look up. Reese is gone. The pond is gone. And so is the ground beneath me.

I am now dangling several feet in the air, alongside the cliff. The red lake roars at me from below as if to say, "The Vsk eagerly awaits you."

The only thing that stands between me and a mangled death is a tree branch that's getting weaker by the moment. I open my mouth to scream but the sound gets caught in my throat, fearing it will somehow cause the branch to break.

Marcus begins his climb down the cliff to rescue me. From above, I see the team looking down at me, horrified. They order me to hold on and not look down. I want to do as they say but my fingers are sweaty, making it hard to maintain a good grip on the branch.

The wind laughs in my ear and whistles a tune dedicated to my demise. I silently beg the branch to ignore the wind and hold steady.

"I'm almost there. *Don't let go,*" he begs me.

I look up and he's climbing down to me as fast as he can, but it's not fast enough. The branch snaps and I plummet to my death…

BOOK 2:
MARCUS CANE

—Lord Byron

CHAPTER TWELVE: THE GAME

Rio approaches me a few minutes after Emmy leaves me standing on the edge of the cliff. I know he's reading my Wave and sometimes I wish I could turn him off.

"What?" I snap.

"I thought I'd check on you before you used your fist to take down the mountain. So, what's up?"

"Well, about five minutes ago, my girlfriend handed me a miniature Spiderman action figure and made me promise to kill her."

"What did you say?"

"I told her sure, no problem," I reply harshly. "How could she ask that of me?"

"I don't think that's what's pissing you off."

"Okay, then why am I pissed?"

"Because you realize she's right. The entire human race matters more than just one person. Even if that person is the girl you love."

"Does your power ever irritate *you?* Because right now it's annoying the hell out of me."

"You have no idea."

"The more she pushes for me to take her life if we don't get the Amulet, the more I want to fight for her. How is it fair to destroy someone so self-sacrificing?"

"Marcus, there may be a way to get into the castle without having to go into the lake," Isabelle calls out to me.

I rush off and follow her into the cave. We pass Emmy and Jay, who seem intent on watching our every move. Isabelle has listed several books that mention an entrance into the castle. Jay is right, that girl reads too much.

But she's also the reason we may actually get inside of Kairo's castle; that makes her more than okay in my book.

"There was a researcher friend of mine who wrote a book about the relationship between Kairo and his mother. In it he states that although the two are estranged, they often think alike."

"So, he might have modeled Pyron after Difi?" I ask.

"Not in an obvious way, but like Lucy, Kairo would have made sure that if he was ever in danger…"

"He had more than one exit," I reply, finishing her thought.

We scour her well-written notes in search of more clues. She looks across the cave to where Jay and Emmy sit studying us.

"Is he always like this?" she asks me while eyeing Jay.

"Like what?"

"Nice."

"Yeah."

"I guess everyone is at first."

"No, Jay's the real deal."

"How come he doesn't have a girl?"

"He's not really into commitment."

"Oh."

I can actually feel her disappointment fill the space between us.

"Every guy isn't a 'commitment guy' at first, Isabelle. Then we find a girl who is worth it and we don't mind being committed. In fact, we insist."

"I just got my Rah back. I don't want to give it away to someone who's not serious."

"The Rah is just a tangible thing. That comes last."

"Meaning?"

"Meaning, I have seen the way you two look at each other. Your heart's gone already. It's just a matter of time until you hand him your Rah. That's the bad part about it."

"What's bad about taking your time?"

"Nothing, normally. But given the duties that go along with being a Guardian, I'm not sure a long courtship is realistic."

"So you think I should just jump in and be with Jay?"

"I think I wasted a lot of time fighting what I felt for Emmy. In the end all I did was piss off my ex and lose precious time."

"There's all sorts of stuff about you guys in the Splash. I'm not really sure what to believe."

"It's up to you but the Splash isn't with us every day. I'm with Jay most of the time and believe me when I tell you, if he cares about you, then he's in a hundred percent."

She looks over at him as if deliberating on whether or not he's worth taking a chance on. She doesn't tell me what she decides but from the small smile she's suppressing, I would say Jay has a good shot.

When we actually find a possible way into the castle, Emmy and Jay tell us we should let the team Recharge. Normally, we wouldn't need to do that as much as we have been, but being here, so close to Kairo, we have to work harder not to let evil in. That requires us to Recharge more and more.

So Miku is keeping watch outside the cave while everyone rests. I'm about ten minutes into Recharging when I hear Tony-Tone call out my name. I am awake instantly. Right away I see what the cause for alarm is: Emmy is standing in the middle of the cave, eyes open, talking to someone that's not there.

I rush over and call out her name. She doesn't respond. It's as if she doesn't even know I'm there. By now the rest of the team is up. Isabelle calls out Emmy's name too, but Emmy ignores her. After snapping her fingers in front of Emmy's face a few times, Isabelle looks over at me.

"What is it? Why isn't she responding?" I ask.

"I don't know. Does she normally sleepwalk?"

"No, not that I've seen."

Watching my girl have a full-on conversation with someone who isn't really there is freaking me out. I shake her gently but it does nothing to break her out of whatever is happening to her.

"Did she accidently drink some kind of mixture?" I ask Tony.

"I didn't bring anything that could have this effect," Tony says.

"Just give her something to make her wake up," I demand.

"No. If we don't know what's causing her hallucinations, we shouldn't try to treat her. Mixing the wrong mixtures together causes brain damage in humans," Isabelle informs us.

"We need to know what she did today," Jay says.

"She woke up from almost being eaten alive, she interacted with the team, smelled a flower, we talked on top of the cliff…then she came back inside the cave," I recount.

"Tell me about the flower," Isabelle says.

"I don't know—it was just some stupid flower. It had white and black dots. I kept thinking 'it's so like Emmy to find some good in this Omnis-forsaken place.'"

"What she found wasn't good at all. The flower you're describing is called DD: the Deadly Desire rose."

"What does it do besides making her act crazy?" I ask.

"Once she inhaled its scent, it went inside her. Now it's letting her play out her desires. But no matter what the desire is, the ending will always be death. It's the kind of flower that Kairo would have a whole garden of."

"How do we snap her out of it?"

"You don't. You have to let it play out."

"No! I'm not gonna let Emmy stay inside some crazy dream world," I protest.

"Isabelle is right. I know a few Sellers who make a killing harvesting the DDs. You can't wake up from it. You can only hope that you wake up on your own before…ya know," Tony adds.

I watch helpless as Emmy takes off her sneakers and walks out into the forest. The team is right beside me. I keep calling out to her, although they tell me it's useless.

Who is she talking to in her dream? What's happening? Why does she look blissfully happy one minute and worried the next?

Emmy makes her way towards the edge of the cliff. I stand in her way so she doesn't go over. Whoever she's talking to in her mind just made her feel sad again. She turns away from the cliff and starts to head back to the cave.

Isabelle signals to me that that's a good sign; Emmy may be pulling herself out of it.

Chapter Twelve: The Game

Then without the slightest warning, she turns back and leaps off the side of the cliff. It takes a full second for us to realize what Emmy has just done. Everything in me wants to look down and see what happened; at the same time, I dread looking over the edge.

She can't be gone. Not like this…

I look over the side and she's hanging on by a branch. The team is talking to me but I can't hear them. All I know is that I have to go down and get her before she falls. Everything that ever mattered to me is hanging on by a thin branch.

I start to descend down the cliff. I curse Kairo a million times for putting a Vsk at the bottom of the lake and a force field in the air. I can't wait to get this guy. I don't give a damn how the council punishes me.

I'm only a few feet away from her when I hear the sound of wood snapping. It's followed by an earth-shattering cry from below. Emmy has fallen.

There is absolutely no way to explain what I'm feeling when I see her in freefall. It's like someone took the sky away. Nothing makes sense. I don't reflect on the right course of action. I don't stop to consult with the team.

I immediately jump after her. I would rather die knowing I tried to save her than live knowing I didn't.

As soon as I hit the water, the Vsk churns the lake in a funnel-like motion. It pulls me under with its powerful undercurrent. It is almost impossible to see anything other than swirls of discarded angel and human body parts. But if I can somehow spot Emmy, maybe I can get her far enough away so that she can escape. I know the likelihood that she has survived this far is small but I can't give up on her.

The strength of the Vsk nearly pulls my wings apart. I'm going deeper and deeper into the darkness. I fight to keep from being dragged to the floor of the lake, where a mangled future awaits me.

I just need to stay alive long enough to find her.

I swim as far as I can and still no sight of Emmy. I turn the opposite direction and swim out, no sign of her. Finally, I can no longer avoid the Vsk. It pulls me into its center. I'm sucked up into darkness too deep to be natural.

Suddenly, the darkness lifts and I've been washed up onto the center of some kind of platform. Kairo has built the lake with a sublevel that emptiness out into the center of his castle.

Emmy stands wet and shivering a few feet away. I rush over to her, and she latches on to me tightly.

"You know what? That really warms my heart. Well, if I had one," someone says.

I turn and find Kairo a few yards away from me. He isn't what I was expecting. There are no hideous markings on him. He isn't horribly disfigured and doesn't have eyes that swirl with dark abyss. If anything, most people would consider him attractive.

Kairo is about six two. He has mid-length hair, cut into spiky layers. He wears black knee-high leather boots and a button-down red velvet jacket that reaches the floor. He has on dark makeup that accentuates his eyes and red lips. He looks more like a Goth rocker than the son of evil.

I run up to strike him, only to be violently thrown to the floor by a force field. That's when I notice Kairo holding a cane made of "liquid" which stands a few inches off the ground.

"That cane is called a Loop. A Loop is a master key. It controls everything on this side of the force field. Kairo can come in but we can't go out," I inform Emmy in a whisper.

"We have to get the Loop away from him."

"It won't matter. It will only work in Kairo's hand. It won't recognize anyone else's," I reply.

Emmy and I exchange worried looks as Kairo enjoys the sight of his new prisoners trying to figure a way out.

"You need to let us out, Kairo," I order him.

"I'm hurt that you would take that kind of attitude with me. After all, I saved you and the human. Didn't I?" he asks.

"I'm sure you did it because you're a great guy," I retort.

His laugh echoes in the vast castle.

"First, I would like to welcome you to my home. It seems to me that you have gone to a lot of trouble to see me. I didn't want you two to come all this way only to be chewed up by the Vsk. No, that's for everyday beings. Not for my favorite pair of lovers."

Emmy and I are taken aback that he knows who we are.

"Oh yes, I have broken some Splashes. This angel/human love affair is making news everywhere. It seems you two have been a real pain to Lucy."

"You need to let her go, Kairo," I order him.

"Would you like to know more about the Castle Relinque?"

"Let us out!" Emmy shouts.

"If you look around, you'll find some of my most valuable treasures. I think killing with powers or a mixture is too easy. I like the human way: contact with the body," he says pleasantly.

Emmy and I survey the vast room and discover it's a murderer's museum. There's a lengthy display of knives, swords, and torture devices mounted on the wall.

Emmy signals for me to look at the throne Kairo sits on. It's a collection of bones that have been bound together to form the morbid centerpiece of Kairo's lair. He notices Emmy staring at it.

"Do you like my throne? I had a devil of a time putting it together. Alas, I had a lot of help from humans and angels alike," he says smugly.

As he talks, I notice a thick silver necklace with a pendant around his neck. It has the same pattern as that in the book of fairytales. I signal to Emmy and she agrees; Kairo is wearing the Amulet we came for.

"You want to fight me, fine. But Emmy has nothing to do with this," I protest.

"Actually, she is really the only thing that concerns me. See, it's been a long time since I played with a human."

"Don't you touch her!" I shout, placing Emmy protectively behind me.

"She came to my house and now I get to play with her."

"You touch her and I swear to Omnis, I will kill you," I vow.

"Even if you could, my death would be met by yours. The council would have to make it up to Lucy if her son was killed by an angel. You know that."

"I don't care."

"Yes, I sense something very 'hero–like' about you. I hate that," he says.

"Kairo, she's human; there's no sport in killing her."

"Killing her? What do you take me for? I don't just kill like a common everyday demon. My dear friend, I am an artist."

"That means you find ways to make people suffer," Emmy accuses.

"That means if killing people was an actual product, Akons, demons, and Runners would all be PCs. I, dear girl, am a Mac. I kill with power. Precision. Style."

I turn to Emmy and assure her that I will find a way to get her out. She nods but I can see panic behind her eyes.

"What is it that you came for?" Kairo asks.

"You have something that doesn't belong to you," I reply.

"I have several things that don't belong to me. Let's see, I have skulls, ribs, fingers…you're going to have to be more specific."

"The Amulet."

"Oh, this?" he says innocently.

"Yes."

"I knew it had to be important but I never knew why. It was given to me by a Pawn who tried to con me with fake weeping oil. When I found him, he gave me everything he owned. But when it came to this Amulet, he actually tried to keep me from taking it. I promised him that if he handed it over peacefully, I wouldn't kill him. I believe one of the spines glued to the base of my throne is his," he says, looking around to see where he had glued the Pawn's remains.

"You give me the Amulet and we'll leave you alone," I inform him.

"Said the angel behind the force field," Kairo muses.

"I came for the Amulet. I'm going to get it," I promise him.

"I like you, Guardian. In fact, I'll let you in on a little secret most people don't know about me: I'm kind of a geek."

"Yeah, I got that from the PC reference," I retort.

"I mean, I love puzzles. In fact, I have three for you today. And if you and your human solve all three, I will let you choose which blade I fillet your girlfriend with."

"We're not here to play games, Kairo."

"Well, that's good because while this is a game for me, it's incredibly serious for you."

Kairo points the Loop at Emmy and a glass box springs up from the floor and encases her.

"No! Let me be in the box. I'll go in the box. Not her. Leave her alone, you freak!" I protest.

He laughs heartily as he looks on. Emmy examines her glass prison anxiously. She bangs on it repeatedly. I run over to her and try to smash it. I hit the glass with every ounce of strength I have. It has absolutely no impact.

"Here's the deal, Guardian. Your girl is being stripped of oxygen. She can only survive three minutes, at which point, parts of the brain will begin to die. Read the clues engraved on the glass, solve the riddle, and save her."

"Why would you do this?" Emmy screams at Kairo.

"Because, dear, killing outright gets old. When you have the answer, Guardian, just call it out. By the way, you get three guesses. Every time you guess wrong, the air depletes faster."

He points the Loop towards the glass and yells, "Begin!"

CHAPTER THIRTEEN: THIS MUCH I KNOW

Almost immediately, Emmy starts to panic as the air is sucked out of the box. I lean in and reassure her that I will not let anything happen to her. I read the riddle out loud to her so that she can both help and focus on something other than the lack of oxygen.

"What Am I?
I have no legs but I can run
I have no arms but I hang on
I am water that is no longer wet"

"Marcus, I don't know," she says.

"It's okay. Let's think about this for a sec," I reply, trying very hard not to lose it. Then from a few feet away, Kairo begins to laugh.

"She has two minutes and thirty seconds," he says.

Emmy begins to look all over the glass box to try and find some kind of opening. I know right away that will be a waste of precious time.

"Emmy, look at me and nowhere else, okay?"

"Okay."

"What has no legs but can run?" I ask her.

"Time!"

"Yes, time can 'run' out! The answer is 'time,'" I tell Kairo.

He shakes his head and suddenly, Emmy is gasping for air.

"No!" I shout.

"You have two more chances, Guardian," Kairo informs me with delight.

"Don't look at him, Emmy. Focus."

"It's not time…maybe it's…it's…" Her voice is getting weaker. The lack of oxygen will be effecting her brain soon, if not already.

"One minute left," Kairo announces.

"Shut up!" I blare at him. His only reply is to laugh even harder.

"What has no arms?" I say to myself.

"I don't know…can't…think," she whispers. She's turning slightly blue.

"Could he mean the 'hands' of time? No, time is the wrong answer," I say, thinking out loud.

"Sun…chair…go…" Emmy is getting delirious. She has no idea what she's saying now.

"It's the hands of time!" I call out to the demon.

"Wrong again!" he says in a singsong voice.

Emmy's eyes are rolling to the back of her head. I turn away from her, knowing I will never be able to concentrate if I see her withering away. I force myself to focus only on the riddle. I read and reread all the clues. I feel like I'm missing something that's right in front of my face.

Then I look down at the third clue. That's when I realize it's not a clue at all. It's more of an omission. Yes, there's something about the third clue that is going to reveal the answer. I just need to focus in and drown out the steady laughter coming from Kairo.

"Why does it say 'I'm not water'? Is that because it is?" I ask out loud to no one. Emmy is now too weak to remain standing. She slinks down to the bottom of the glass. She is barely conscious.

"Emmy, wake up! Emmy, please wake up!"

"You have ten seconds!" Kairo says with utter glee.

Why does he take the time to point out that it's not water? When is water not really water…? When it's an image of water. An image that "hangs"…on the wall?

Got it! A painting "hangs" on the wall through it has no arms. It's a painting of water, so it's not wet, and what kind of water always runs?

"It's a painting of a waterfall!"

Kairo points the Loop at the glass and Emmy is freed instantly. I quickly get down on the floor and check on her.

"Em, wake up," I beg.

She opens her eyes, shocked that she is now able to breath. She coughs for several minutes. I hold her hand and help her breathe normally.

"So touching. You have ten seconds before the next game," he says.

"Marcus, I don't know if I can do this," she admits.

"You can. I know you can. He's too far away now, but if I can figure a way to get him to come closer to the force field, I can use my power and reflect his fear back to him."

"We're not gonna die here, right?"

"No, baby. We're not," I promise her.

"Okay, folks, now time for round two!" he says, throwing a jagged, crude-looking stick on the floor, towards her.

He tells her to put it in her mouth so that she doesn't swallow her tongue. He doesn't want her to choke on her own blood and that kind of death is too quick.

I don't give a damn what the council does to me. I'm going to end this guy…

"What're you going to do to her now?" I ask.

"It's simply shocking, I tell you." He laughs and points the Loop at her.

The glass box appears. Although this time there is a keypad underneath the riddle.

"Are you suffocating her to death again?" I ask, studying Emmy inside the glass.

"And what, repeat my work? Please, have you ever heard of Mac reissuing products without some delicious new upgrade?" he brags.

"Just tell me what the hell you want me to do," I snap.

"She gets shocked every two minutes she's in the box. That is, until you key in the right five-letter word answer to the riddle engraved above. Other humans have lasted ten rounds. But your human is significantly smaller and weaker. So, I would hurry."

"Fine, anything else?" I ask, trying not to lose my temper, knowing it won't help.

"You only get one chance with this one. If you key in the wrong answer, I'm gonna deep fry her like butter on a stick at the state fair."

I look over at him, perplexed.

"Human activities amuse me," he says.

"Just start," I counter.

"As you wish."

He points the Loop at the glass and the keypad lights up.

"It has the entire alphabet printed on it. Given the number of spaces on the screen, the answer is a five-letter word. There's a timer next to it. It counts down from 120 seconds," I explain to Emmy.

"Read the riddle," she says.

On the Way Home…
A mother is walking home with her 3 children
One is an angel
One is a demon
One is human
She encounters a beast which blocks her path.
The beast demands two of her three children as a sacrifice.
Who makes it home?
? ? ? ? ?

As soon as I am done reading the riddle, I look over at the timer and we have only ten seconds before Emmy will be shocked. She reads the expression on my face and tears flood into her eyes.

"Let me do it, Kairo. Let me be in the box!"

Emmy shakes her head. Kairo just laughs and says he's having too much fun to switch victims.

She looks as me with sheer terror as she puts the stick in her mouth. The timer is down to three seconds. We look at each other knowing nothing can stop what's about to take place.

The timer hits zero.

The jolt of electricity rips through her body. She convulses uncontrollably from side to side. Her jaw clenches and drool drips down the side of her face. Enraged, I bang on the glass and curse Kairo. I vow to the heavens that I will kill him.

The electricity stops just as easily as it came on. The timer starts up again and gives us two minutes.

She falls to the bottom of the glass box and weeps heavily. I tell her I'm sorry this is happening but that I will get her out. She looks up at me and tells me she's okay.

I'm okay until I spot that her fingers are now a morose blue-black color and blood is dripping from her nose to the front of her shirt.

"Read," she begs me. I pull myself together and reread the riddle. Emmy thinks hard and replies:

"Okay, okay. The mother gave two of her children away. Which one would she have held on to? Is it the angel? Or the demon?" she says.

"I would say the angel but then again, we have to consider who's asking the question. It's from a demon, so in his eyes, the child that should be kept is the demon, right?"

"Yeah, I guess."

"Emmy, we can't guess! We only have one shot. If we're wrong…"

The timer reads five seconds.

"I'm not sure. Maybe it's the human?" she says.

"They're all five-letter words. It could be any—"

The timer is down to zero.

She doesn't even have time to put the stick in her mouth before the bastard turns the electricity back on with the Loop. Immediately, Emmy's body violently jerks around like a fish ripped from the water and flung onto a fisherman's boat.

A small river of blood leaps from her mouth onto the floor of the glass box. I smell urine and searing flesh. Emmy has lost control of her bladder and there are welts all over her. The girl I love is being cooked within her own skin.

The timer starts up again and gives us two minutes.

"I'm gonna tell him we'll do whatever he wants. I can't let this happen to you," I plead with her.

She crawls up to the glass and whispers something to me.

"Are you sure?" I ask her. She nods yes.

The timer gives us five more seconds.

I do as she says. I go up to the keypad and press the keys that spell out:

"No one"

The timer goes off. Nothing happens. Emmy had the right answer. Kairo stands up and is livid.

"How the hell did you guess that?" he demands.

"Get her out of the damn box!" I scream.

He uses the Loop and the glass box disappears into the floor.

Angry, Kairo gets up from his throne and takes a step closer to the force field. Then he uses his powers. He can move things like Ameana can but his ability is far more advanced. He lifts Emmy into the air with just his index finger, and without touching her, he is able to force her tospread her arms and legs out wide so he can examine her. He rotates her three hundred and sixty degrees.

"What are you?" he shouts.

I yell at him to put her down. He warns me if I interfere, he'll kill her on the spot. Then with the slightest move of his little finger, he slices Emmy open.

In complete horror, I gasp her name.

"Relax, she's in suspended animation. She can't feel anything. At least not until I begin the third game."

"Put her down!" I demand.

"I just want to see if she's really human. She has freaky eyes and she's been able to withstand more than most. And she knew the answer to a riddle that no one else was able to guess."

Kairo slides Emmy's heart, lungs, and kidneys out of her body and over a few feet to the left. It's like he's playing some bizarre touch screen game where he can add or remove organs from his victims as he sees fit. Emmy's eyes are open but she seems frozen.

Moments later, Kairo puts all her organs back inside her body and she falls to the floor. I rush to her side.

"How did you know the answer was 'no one'?" he asks her again.

Then Emmy does something so strange, at first I thought my girl had truly lost her mind. She starts laughing at the son of all things evil. Her laughter is hysterical and filled with delight.

"You dare laugh at me? I will break you, human!" Kairo vows.

She laughs harder and whispers to me to get ready. I nod although I'm not really sure what's going on.

"How did I guess your stupid little riddle?" she asks in a small, cracked voice.

"Tell me!" Kairo orders.

"Marcus told me to think about the person telling the riddle. That's when I remembered that this is all about you. You're nothing but a mama's boy." She laughs again.

He walks even closer to us. And now I understand what Emmy is trying to do: lure Kairo closer so I can use my powers on him.

"What did you say to me, human?" Kairo asks venomously.

"You're a mama's boy. All this is about you missing your mommy. You called the castle 'abandon.' I thought you were talking about leaving hope behind. But that's not it at all. You call it that because Lucy made you, then discarded you like trash. She abandoned you."

"She only sent me away because the council forced her to."

"Please, she's the source of all evil. She could have fought for you but she didn't and you want to know why?"

"I am going to kill you. It will be slower than I have ever killed anyone. You will beg me to end your life!"

"Blah, blah. Do you what human trait Lucy created you with?"

"No one knows what the human factor was."

"I do—love. She knew you'd be powerful. She created you, so that was a given. But she didn't want you to ever overthrow her. That's why she gave you something she doesn't have: the ability to desire love. That way she would always be able to defeat you."

"I will break every bone inside you and feed it to you," he promises her.

"That's why the answer to the riddle is 'no one.' Because the mother in the story loved her children so much, she would rather the beast kill all of them than abandon any of them. That is unlike your mother. Wow, how much do you have to suck for your own mom to give you away?"

"I'm going to cut inside you and display your remains on my wall."

"Here's what you and your dumbass mother don't understand: while love destroys you, it'll keep humanity going forever."

Chapter Thirteen: This Much I Know

"ARGH!!!" He runs into the force field, Loop in hand.

He's so focused on killing Emmy he doesn't even see me coming toward him. By the time he does, it's too late. I grab hold of his neck and bash his head into the floor. The Loop falls beside him. Before he can counterattack, I look him in the eyes and reflect his fear back to him.

It is much more difficult to penetrate Kairo's fears than a normal demon's. It requires more concentration. He's trying to block me out of his mind. I call out to Emmy and tell her she has to get out in case Kairo breaks free.

"I can't, the force field is still up. Anyone can get in but getting out, I need the Loop. And only Kairo's hand can use it," she protests.

"Find a way, quickly," I warn her. It gets harder and harder to control my reflecting powers.

Emmy looks around and spots the stick she was forced to bite on. She goes over to it and without the slightest hesitation, sinks the sharp edge into Kairo's wrist.

Kairo screams so loud, it echoes back to us endlessly. Emmy looks like she's about to throw up as she severs Kairo's hand from the rest of his body with the crude instrument. Unable to completely take it apart, she stomps on it with her foot until the hand is no longer attached.

As Kairo yells and curses, black oil-like blood seeps from his bloody stub. He's lost focus, so reflecting his fear back at him is getting much easier now. I enjoy going further and further into the abyss of his psyche. I will render him no more threatening than a newborn.

Emmy bends down, grabs the hand, and picks up the Loop with it. She holds it out in front of her. She finds the other piece of the stick and hurls it across the room to see if the force field is gone. The stick lands on the throne: the force field has broken.

There is nothing Kairo can do now because I am in control. As he struggles under the weight of my power, Emmy calmly climbs to the top of the throne and reaches for one of Kairo's knives.

"Marcus, you are forbidden to kill him," Emmy reminds me.

Kairo is gasping for his last breath but even then he manages a sneaky little smile, knowing I can't kill him without incurring the wrath of the council.

Emmy bends down and addresses Lucy's son.
"I have a riddle for you," she says.
He looks up at her with disgust. She leans in real close and smiles.
"What has one hand, two legs, and won't ever finish?"
"I don't kn—"
She sinks the knife into his chest.

CHAPTER FOURTEEN: STRENGTH IN WEAKNESS

After I pull the Amulet off Kairo's neck, we make our way outside the castle. The team is approaching and Ameana is among them. Seeing the state Emmy is in, Tony goes into his knapsack and tries to find something that will help her.

She is still shaking, badly bruised and very weak. So weak in fact, she passes out as Tony examines her. Isabelle advises us to let Emmy rest while they extract various plant mixtures to treat her.

In the meantime, I recount the events to the team. I leave out the part about Emmy urinating because I know she'd want me to, although I'm sure the team figured it out. The Fire Swans are now flying over to the castle. Apparently the force field over the lake is down as well.

When it's time to go, I ask Rio to carry Emmy as I have yet to gain back my full strength. A few hours later, we stop at a hotel, where Emmy takes a hot shower. Miku insists that Emmy go shopping as well.

"No, let's just grab a maid's uniform from the cart in the lobby. We don't have time to shop," I remind Miku.

"There is always time to shop." Miku, Ameana, and Isabelle all correct me.

I look to Rio for his help but he agrees with the girls.

"It'll take fifteen minutes," he says.

The guys wait while the girls go inside a small shop and pick out a few items. What was supposed to be fifteen minutes is actually an hour and a half. But I didn't complain because, well, when you get electrocuted repeatedly, the least your boyfriend can do is wait while you shop.

When Emmy comes out of the store she has on new clothes, smells like spring flowers, and the color is slowly coming back to her face. I hold her close and ask how she is feeling.

"The way any girl would feel after taking down a super demon—hungry," she says.

I hold her tighter than I should given what she's just been through.

"That was…close," I whisper to her.

"Very."

Next, we drop off Tony and Isabelle before we head to Adam City. Although Tony doesn't say it out loud, I can read the relief on his face when he lands safely on the ground.

"Hey, thank you for helping us," Rio says to him.

"You showed a lot of courage for a Seller," Ameana agrees.

"It was nothing. I was never scared."

We all look at each other and agree to let Tony think whatever he wanted. After all, he was instrumental in us getting the Amulet. He saved us with his mixtures and his knowledge of the market.

"You guys wanna stick around for a little while?" he asks eagerly.

"We have one other matter to see to," I respond.

"Oh yeah, the secret part of the mission," he replies.

"Yeah, kind of," Emmy replies.

We turn to leave when he calls us back.

"Hey, you remember the story I told you guys earlier?" he asks.

"You mean about your best friend?"

"Yeah, could we keep that just between us?"

We all agree to do as he asks.

"I don't feel bad about it or anything. I mean it was a long time ago. Who really remembers their human lives anymore, right?" he says, mostly to himself.

Then Emmy walks up to him and hugs him. He's surprised by her affection but returns it nonetheless.

"You were closed for days. You lost a lot of business," Isabelle observes.

"Oh well," he says.

The team exchanges a glance and decides to help Tony out. The twins buy mixtures and Holders they don't really need. Ameana buys Samson string, and Jay and Isabelle look for something to purchase as well. Emmy takes my hand and we quietly sneak out of the shop and into the alley.

"Are you sure you're alright?" I ask her again.

"I think I need to sleep for a year but yeah, I'm fine."

"We survived it."

She bursts into tears so suddenly, it startles me.

"Emmy, what is it?"

"Nothing. I'm just so happy we made it. For a second there, I wasn't so sure."

"So these are tears of happiness?"

"Yeah."

"Good, but I'm still not a fan of seeing you in tears. Happy or not."

"Sorry."

She wipes her face and holds on to me tightly.

She asks me what caused her to end up on the side of the cliff. I fill her in on the flower and its effect. She scolds herself for doing something so reckless.

"It's okay, you were just trying to find something good in the middle of all the darkness that surrounded us. I can't blame you for that," I tell her.

"Still, I'm done smelling flowers."

"Who did you see in your hallucination?"

"Reese."

"Oh, but you looked sad. I would have thought seeing Reese again would have made you happy."

"Yeah, it did. But he started telling me stuff…"

"What stuff?" I ask.

"He told me how he kind of liked me."

"So Reese saw you as the girl that got away."

"I guess."

"What about you, is he the guy that got away from you?"

"What do you mean?"

I mean would the two of you be together now if he hadn't died?

"Never mind," I say out loud.

"Marcus, what is it?" she asks.

"How often is Reese on your mind?"

"We were friends."

"That's not an answer."

"I think about him once in a while."

"He kissed you."

"That was a long time ago. Anyway, he's gone now."

"I don't want to be the guy you settle for."

"Seriously, Marcus? I was the one who made the first move. Do you remember that? Do you remember your ex smashing my head against the wall because I asked you out?"

"Maybe you and Reese were…closer than you and I are," I reply, looking away from her.

She repositions herself so that she is right in front of me and there is no way to avoid eye contact with her. She places her hand on either side of my face.

"Marcus, you and I can't get any closer. You live in the spaces between my breath, my heartbeat, and my thoughts."

"Are you sure no part of you wanted Reese?"

"I'm your girl. Nothing, *nothing* will change that. Got it?"

"Yeah, I got it."

"Good, now shut up and kiss me."

I do as I'm told. Jay and Isabelle exit the shop and find us kissing. Jay clears his throat, loudly.

"Can we save the girl's life before you make out with her?" he asks.

"I think it's romantic," Isabelle replies.

"Please, Marcus's romance game is weak compared to mine," Jay insists.

"Oh, really?" she challenges.

"Yeah, if you behave, I'll show you what I mean."

"Are you asking me out again?" she says.

"Maybe."

"I'm sorry, I'm gonna need a solid yes or no."

I like this girl…

Looking at Emmy, she too approves of Isabelle's hard stand with Jay.

"Okay, fine. I'm asking you. There. Happy?"

"Yeah, you're a real romantic, Jay," Emmy mocks.

He ignores her and addresses Isabelle.

"So…what do you say?" he pushes.

"Yes, I will go out with you."

"Yeah boy, I knew I was in there!" he shouts as he takes her into his arms and lifts her up high in the air. Isabelle is completely caught off guard.

"Okay, but you have to meet my family. We're very close. And they *have* to like you," she tells him.

"Then you have to meet Siren, my car. And you best believe she has to approve of you," Jay counters.

"Again, Jay, it's not right to base your feelings on a car," Emmy says, shaking her head.

"Well, it depends on the car. Is it a V6 or V8?" she asks him. Jay doesn't answer. He's too taken aback by her question.

"What's the difference?" Emmy asks.

"Simple: The V6 has six cylinders while the V8 has eight cylinders. But while the V8 is stronger, it uses more far more gas. Now if you're talking about an SUV, well, that's different—"

"You know cars?"

"Yeah."

"It's like we're two halves of a whole, baby!" he says to her proudly.

Jay is officially off the market…

"C'mon, Emmy, let's go get this Dy cast out of you cuz I got business to handle," Jay says, looking suggestively at Isabelle.

"I couldn't agree more," a sinister voice replies. We all look up and find Frenzy in the air. He's surrounded by the three remaining Akons: Mayhem, Chaos, and their leader, Rage.

The rest of the Guardians appear just as Frenzy shoots his first bolt of lightning. Fearful of what will happen if I leave her on the ground, I grab Emmy and take off into the sky. The Akons furiously follow. Jay tells Isabelle to make a break for it and head home but she refuses to leave.

We're now flying above Rockefeller Center, where a massive Christmas tree has been erected. The holiday lights give the city a soft, warm glow. But all the beauty is lost as Akons and Guardians battle for what each side knows could be the very last time.

Frenzy throws a lightning bolt at Miku. It catches her off guard and she drops from the sky like a broken-winged bird. I place Emmy on the roof of a nearby skyscraper and dive to get Miku. I catch her just as she is about to hit the ground.

Rage, focused on getting to Emmy, dives down into the skyscraper and blasts her full on with a fireball. I'm too far away to reach her. Rio gets there just in time to use his shield and block Rage's attack.

Ameana calls for the windshield wiper from a car below. It comes to her and she uses it as a makeshift knife. She sends it right at Frenzy's chest. The speed it's traveling makes it a lethal blow. Unfortunately, Frenzy turns away in time so the blow isn't fatal, but it does puncture his right eye. Frenzy cries out in agony as he pulls the weapon from his eye socket. He curses, moans, and calls Ameana every name there ever was. Then he takes to the air to kill her.

Meanwhile, I order Emmy to run but Rage blocks her path down the street. I try to rush over to her, only to have Mayhem's dagger tear through my right leg. I pull out the blade before the poison has time to set in.

Unfortunately, though, the delay gives Rage a chance to attack Emmy. He leaps out and tackles her. They both fall to the ground.

"Tonight you die, human," Rage vows venomously. He pins her down on the floor, grabs her throat, and tries to squeeze the breath out of her. I'm about to take off and help her when Chaos sends a mob of holiday shoppers to slow me down. It works. The humans are pushing and kicking me with whatever they can find.

Trying to stop them and not hurt any of them makes this a difficult obstacle. Normally with this many humans around, the Akons would never attack, but they are getting desperate. This is the last few days they have to obtain the Triplex.

Miku manages to yank a few of them off me. Ameana sends some of them flying into the big Christmas tree. If we are any more aggressive, the humans will be severely hurt.

Isabelle goes over to Emmy as Rage is about to scoop her eyes out with his bare hands. She grabs a string of Christmas lights from the tree, ties it around Rage's neck, and is able to yank him off of her. But Rage is far stronger and in seconds he manages to get out from Isabelle's hold.

Frenzy, fuming that Emmy has gotten away, blasts Jay with a series of lightning bolts. But Jay is too fast even for the lightning. When he is at a safe distance, Jay turns to Frenzy to gloat. But there is an unexpected look on the Akon's face. Frenzy is looking down on the ground a few yards from me with a look of pure joy.

Jay turns to see what Frenzy's looking at: Isabelle is writhing in pain on the ground. One of the bolts hit her in the abdomen. Jay looks horrified.

The twins reassure him that they have Isabelle and they will shield her. Jay looks at Frenzy with renewed hatred. He Glides over to confront him. Ameana goes up to the roof to help Jay.

"No, Frenzy will die by my hands," Jay promises. Ameana wisely steps back.

They two of them tackle each other and trade blows. The entire building shakes every time they collide. Eventually Frenzy gets the better of Jay and continues to pound on him. Not satisfied, Frenzy gets close to a lifeless Jay, stands over him, and lifts his arms up to fire the final bolt of lightning.

"I'm gonna remember this for the rest of my life," Frenzy says with a sneer.

Jay, having only *pretended* to be immobile, springs up and Glides behind Frenzy with speed I didn't know he was capable of. It takes Frenzy a few seconds to register that his victim now has the advantage.

"You're a bad boy, Frenzy, time to take your toys away," Jay says sweetly.

He then grabs both of Frenzy's hands, pulls his arms backwards, and pops them out of their sockets. The cry coming from Frenzy echoes throughout the city of New York. Jay plants his foot between Frenzy's shoulder blades and literally rips both arms off. Frenzy dies instantly.

Meanwhile, Chaos decides not only to send shoppers to attack us, but to mind control them into hurting themselves. We have to pry them away from oncoming traffic and rooftops. He does all of this just to keep us distracted.

The only way to stop the crowd is to take Chaos out, but I can't find him anywhere. I call out to the rest of the team and Rio tells me Chaos is halfway down the street. Of course he is. That coward wants to keep a safe distance. I take to the air and find the little weasel.

He doesn't see me coming. He's too focused on the anarchy he is causing. I grab him by the throat and hurl him through the wall of a nearby building. He tries to get up. I'm on him before he can get very far.

I stand over him and reflect his worst fear back to him. He tries to break free of me but I'm much too strong for him. In all his jerky, wild movements, he accidently latches on to the Amulet around my neck. Then I make a mistake: I show him the Amulet matters.

It was a simple gesture—I inhaled sharply. But while Chaos is a coward, he's no fool. He knows that for some reason this Amulet is important but he doesn't know why. He hurls the Amulet across the street.

I run to retrieve it, only to be stopped by Rage, who gets to it first. Rage studies it and asks why it's so important. I don't answer.

"See, that's the problem. You don't know how to communicate. You can really hurt a relationship. I bet that's what happened with you and Ameana. Or wait, was it something else? Were you unable to satisfy her, Marcus? Is that why you had to go to a human? You weren't strong enough to handle a real angel?" Rage says, trying to provoke me.

"Rage, if you hand it over, I won't kill you tonight. I promise."

"Big words for the guy whose guts I'm gonna make into barbecue."

"Rage, I really don't want to tell you again. Hand over the Amulet."

"Why is this so important?"

"You have until the count of three," I warn him.

"Well sure, I can hand it over; if you hand me the girl."

"Never gonna happen."

"So you would rather have the girl?"

"One."

"Let me ask you something. When I carve your girlfriend's eyes and scrape out the map, what should I do with her remains?"

"Two."

"I got it! I'm gonna make her into confetti. You know, for the New Year's Eve celebration. What do you think?"

"Three."

"So what, Marcus? What are you gonna—" Before he can finish his sentence, Miku has latched herself on to him and is singing him a sweet melody. The song can't kill Rage but it can inflict massive amounts of pain.

Chapter Fourteen: Strength in Weakness

Rage tries to stop himself from peeling his own skin off like all of Miku's victims do when she sings to them.

I grab the Amulet just as Rage forms a Powerball. I warn Miku just in time; she lets go of him and takes off into the air. I turn as Chaos tries to flee the scene. I launch into the sky and pull him back down to the ground.

"I wasn't done with you yet," I inform the Akon.

I ram him up against the wall and whisper quietly in his ear.

"You should never piss off a guy who knows all your fears."

Then I reflect his nightmares back to him. The magnitude of his fear causes him to tremble and weep openly. I think about the number of humans that Chaos has killed by taking control of their minds. That thought causes me to redouble my efforts. I am the last thing Chaos sees before his death.

A block away, I spot Mayhem. His face is contorted in anger. I'm guessing he just learned from Rage that they are the only two Akons remaining. Mayhem looks around for a way to retaliate. Luckily, Emmy is nowhere to be found. Unfortunately, there is another being near enough to him that he can exact his revenge on.

Ameana Jones is about to die. There is no other way this can play out. There are no Guardians close enough to stop Mayhem's attack. Ameana is too busy helping one of Chaos's victims. She will not turn in time to see the daggers coming at her.

Jay and I make eye contact; the blades are already midway to Ameana. The twins look up and at once they come to the same conclusion I have: no one can stop Mayhem in time. Is it better that she doesn't see it coming?

Ameana props the human up against the wall. She then turns and finds her life, once again, at an end. But somehow, someone close to her stands in the way of the knives. Someone used their own body as a shield, preventing Ameana's doom.

"Rage!" Ameana calls out, shocked, as the wounded Akon hits the ground. We all make our way towards them.

Mayhem, as confused as the rest of us, charges towards Rage. He doesn't get far. Rage sends a fireball into Mayhem's chest. Mayhem dies instantly.

Ameana goes over to the last surviving Akon. Rage has been stabbed once in the shoulder and twice on his right side.

He signals for Ameana to come closer. She leans in and he whispers something in her ear. Then he struggles and pulls out a Port from his pocket. The Port unfolds itself. Rage slinks onto it and disappears.

When we all reach Ameana, the shock had not worn off. She tells us what the last remaining Akon whispered in her ear.

"'I did it because I love you. That doesn't mean I'm good, it just means I'm weak.'"

CHAPTER FIFTEEN: MOST BEAUTIFUL

After Jay says goodbye to Isabelle, we take off to Adam City. The journey is filled with reflective silence. The sight of an Akon risking his life for an angel is something that has never taken place in the history of good and evil.

It weighs heavily on the team's mind, but the person it has the most effect on is Ameana. She looks distant and perplexed. I can't imagine what she's feeling. On one hand, Rage would murder her entire team with no hesitation if he ever got the chance. But on the other hand, the certainty with which he saved her life was nothing short of…Para-worthy selflessness.

Rage's actions aren't the only reason for the thick silence. This is the moment we have all been waiting for. If everything goes right, we should be able to save both the world and Emmy. We're standing on the brink of a long-sought-after victory. It's as if speaking will somehow jinx all our efforts. So we fly in silence.

So much has happened since we first landed on Earth, I fear there will be yet another complication. But according to the sisters, all we have to do is hand over the Amulet. Then we get to save both the world and Emmy. It's like winning the lotto. You know there is always a chance it could happen but when it actually does, you check the numbers a million times.

We had no problem getting past the Tics. Lakom was standing by with a Port. We got on before they could start chasing us. Once inside the temple, we're greeted by the triplets.

"I trust you were successful," Chance says confidently.

"We have it. But you need to cast the Dy out of Emmy first," I order.

"No, first you hand over the Amulet," she insists.

"That's not how it works," Ameana says.

"Okay, guys, let's all just calm down. Chance, you have our word. After you help Emmy, we'll give you the Amulet," Rio promises.

"I think that sounds okay," Charity says to her sisters.

"Fine," Choice agrees with great reluctance.

A long dark table with restraints on the side appears out of nowhere. They instruct Emmy to lie down. She looks over at me. I signal to her that it's okay. She goes over to the table and lies across it.

"What are you going to do to her?" I ask.

"We're going to insert this needle in her eye. There's a mixture inside it that will break the map into hundreds of tiny specks. Then it will collect each speck individually and transfer them from the human's eye into the tube," Chance explains.

The needle she's using is as thin as an eyelash. Its tip is gold colored and extends out into a long, thin translucent tube.

"Is it going to hurt?" I ask.

"Yes."

"You never said anything about pain," I protest.

"We're trying to remove an item that's been embedded inside her eyes for years. It's deep in her cells. How could it not hurt?" Choice says testily.

"We're not gonna let you torture her," Jay says.

"From what I understand, she's used to that," Choice replies smugly.

Seriously, what is this chick's problem?

"Marcus, I can handle it," Emmy says, looking up at the ceiling.

"How bad is it going to be?" I ask.

"Not as bad as ripping through her eye socket," Chance replies as she heads toward the table.

"How long will it take?" Ameana asks.

"The entire night."

"Okay, I'll stay with her," I inform her.

"Impossible. I need to concentrate," Chance replies.

"I'm not leaving her."

"Do you understand that even the slightest interruption can render her blind for the rest of her life? That is *if* she lives?"

"Your father did this to all of you?" I ask.

"Yes, he did," they answer all at once.

I hate that.

"And how were you able to endure?" Miku inquires.

"Simple. He taught us at an early age that love is pain. I would think the human would know that since that's what loving you has brought her so far," Choice says.

I exchange a look with Jay and he, too, is baffled by Choice's reaction towards me. Ameana is enjoying this moment, although she's polite enough to try and hide it.

"The sooner we do this, the sooner we get our freedom. So please, leave the room so we can begin," Chance orders us.

"I'm not gonna let her get hurt again," I inform them.

"I'm sorry, I was under the impression you had no other option. Has an option presented itself since we last spoke?"

"No."

"Then can we get on with it?"

I look around the room and the team seems to agree; there is no other way.

I go over and take Emmy's hand in mine.

"Don't worry. I'll be fine," she says.

"I think I'm supposed to be giving you the pep talk here."

"Oh, so you've done this before?" she jokes.

"Can you guys give us a minute?" I ask the others. Chance is about to object but then she thinks better of it and she ushers everyone out.

Once we're alone, Emmy sits up.

"You don't have to be brave for me. It's okay if you're scared," I tell her.

"Listen, it sounds like there's a chance something could go wrong," she cautions me.

"Nothing is gonna go wrong."

"Just listen, if it does, you have to make sure they keep going. The map is more important than me. Remember you promised, right?"

"Yeah, I remember."

"And if I don't make it, give Ms. Charlotte to Ben. She really likes him. Tell Uncle Max that I love him. Tell the team…thank you. And when you start blaming yourself, like I know you will…remember, I would do it all over again," she says, beaming.

I gently pull her towards me and kiss her deeply, desperately, and maybe for the last time. A rush of longing flows through me. It's only then that I realize it's not about wanting Emmy. It's about *needing* her.

Dear Omnis, I need her. I need her. I need her…

All too soon there is a knock on the door. It's time to let Chance and her sisters cast the Dy out of Emmy. I didn't think I would ever dread anything more than knowing she's going to suffer…

The sisters enter and signal that it's time for me to leave. I kiss my girl on the forehead and tell her that I'll see her soon. She smiles sadly, traces my lips with her fingers, then lies down on the table.

As I walk by Chance, I address her in a steely tone.

"If she dies, you die."

The minute she screams, I run to break the door down and go get her. Jay Glides ahead to me. The screaming coming from the room is far worse than back in the castle because unlike the castle, I've actually given permission for her to be tortured.

"Move," I order him.

"Yo, you need to be cool."

"You need to get out of my way," I warn.

She screams again.

"Jay, move!"

"Marcus, if you enter now, you could cause Chance to lose focus and injury Emmy."

"You could do much worse than injure her," Rio says.

She screams again. Each time her voice cuts me to my soul.

"She needs me."

"What she needs is for you to stay out here," Miku says gently.

Emmy screams again. I put my fist through the opposite wall. The cracks spread down the corridor.

"Marcus, enough, let's take a walk," Ameana says.

"No. I'm not leaving her."

"I'm not asking. I'm telling you," she says coldly.

"Who are you to command me?"

"I'm the second in charge. And when the first guy in charge is punching walls, I have the right to request we meet in private and discuss the situation."

"Fine," I snap. I follow her to the garden. Emmy's cries get further away but I can still hear her.

"What is it?" I ask her impatiently.

"Is this the way you're being strong for her, falling apart?"

"You don't understand—"

"Why? Because I don't cry every second of the day? Marcus, I know more about hurt and loss than you can even begin to understand. You need to stay focused."

"What if she doesn't survive this?"

"Your girlfriend has a lot of issues. But she doesn't give up. She keeps going. She's like a really annoying rash that won't go away. No matter how many times you try to get rid of it," she says, almost to herself.

"So you and Emmy will never get along even after everything?"

"No."

"I get along with Wolf."

"Please, Wolf gets along with demons, Sellers, telemarketers…"

I laugh despite myself. Then Emmy does something that Ameana and I both know will cause me to stop the procedure: she calls out for me.

"Marcus, Marcus, help me. Help me!"

Ameana wisely steps in front of me. She's about to argue but before she speaks, I back down, knowing she's right.

"Okay." I relent, pacing up and down the garden.

I run my hands through my hair as if it will make this all go away. Then something happens that's almost as startling as Rage doing a good deed: my ex-girlfriend reaches out for me.

Her embrace feels warm, welcoming, and familiar. The intoxicating scent of her hair causes my mind to flash back to another time. Back when we used to playfully chase each other across continents. Back when we shared ideas and inner thoughts.

Back when we shared kisses and so much more…

We slowly pull apart from the embrace. But the distance between us is too small for angels who are just friends. I step back.

"I…I should get inside…" I say apologetically.

"Yeah, okay," she says.

I rush back to the temple. Before I can open the door, Ameana calls out to me.

"Marcus?"

"Yeah?"

"Nothing…" she says with a sad smile.

I head back inside where I belong.

The next few hours are a hell that mankind can't begin to understand. Finally, I see the sunrise through the windows.

"It's morning," I announce, still unable to stop pacing.

"How long has it been since she last cried out?" Rio says.

"It's been forty-six minutes and twenty-seven seconds," I inform them.

As much as her cries pain me, they let me know she's alive. So her being silent makes me wonder if something didn't go horribly wrong.

Miku comes over and rests against me.

"She's gonna be okay, Marcus. It's almost over," she assures me.

"Actually, it's over," Rio says.

I ask him if he's certain and he tells us Emmy's Wave is reading "relieved."

I slowly enter the room. Chance tells me it's okay to come all the way inside.

"How is she?" I ask.

"Weak, but otherwise okay."

Chapter Fifteen: Most Beautiful

I go over to her and stroke her hair. Her eyes are still closed. She moans softly.

I can't make out what she's saying.

"Emmy, what is it?"

"I deserve ice cream," she says in a hoarse whisper.

"Okay, babe." I shake my head as relief makes its way down my wings.

"Big. Big. Ice cream," she adds.

"You got it," I assure her.

"Baby girl, I'm proud of you," Jay tells her.

"Thanks, Jay. What happens now?"

"We release all the specks that have gathered in the tube. The map should reassemble itself once it hits that air," Charity says.

"Since the Triplex was found by good, there should be a light that breaks into the sky. That light will summon the reflection of three Original Paras. Each one represents a council member. Then the map will go into oblivion for another six hundred sixty-six years," Rio tells her.

"There's only one possible problem," Chance says.

Of course there is…

"What?" I ask, growing angrier because once again, the sisters withheld something from us.

"If we missed even one speck from the human's eyes, the map will be incomplete and the Para reflections won't appear," Choice says.

"Does that mean the Dy will be cast back inside me?"

"Yes, Emmy," Charity says regretfully.

"The only thing to do is cast it out onto the sky and see if all three Paras appear," Chance says, as if it's no big deal.

So far, I'm not loving the Quo people…

"If you missed a speck or two, we do this all over again?" Ameana asks.

"No. The human will not survive another attempt," Chance tells us.

"Why the hell didn't you mention all this to us in the beginning?" I bark.

"Marcus, calm down," Rio says.

"No, he's right. You three are full of secrets. What else are you hiding?" Jay asks.

"We should ask the same of you. Where is our Amulet?" Choice says.

"You get it if, and only if, this works," I reply.

"Look, let's just gather the specks and see what happens," Charity reasons with the group.

"This better work," I caution the three of them.

The triplets gather the tube and head outside. I help Emmy off the table and we all join the sisters in the garden. I look in Emmy's eyes and although the map isn't there anymore, her eyes are still a vivid purple.

They prick the tube with the point of the needle. Gold specks leap out and take to the air. We wait with bated breath as the specks take the shape of the map and ascend to the sky.

Emmy takes my hand. Rio places his hand on Jay's shoulder.

"Reese died so we could get to this moment," Miku says softly. Ameana takes her hand. The map is so far up, it's now the size of a star.

Nothing happens.

I tell the group to wait a little while longer.

Nothing happens.

Emmy squeezes my hand tighter and tells everyone to give it a few more seconds.

Nothing happens.

"Oh no," Miku moans.

Then, a Para is reflected in the sky.

We're all frozen with anticipation as we pray for Para number two.

The second Para appears.

"Yes!" Jay shouts.

"Shhhh," Rio says as we look around for the third and final Para.

We wait.

We wait.

We wait.

Nothing happens.

"DAMN IT!" I shout, turning away from the sky.

"Marcus—" Emmy begins.

"No, this is wrong. After everything—"

"Marcus—"

"No, don't tell me to calm down. This is crap!"

"Marcus!"

Chapter Fifteen: Most Beautiful

"WHAT???"

She points her index finger towards the sky. And there, standing in a pool of brilliant light, is the third Para. The light from all three bathes the entire sky.

We rejoice so loud, we scare every living thing in the garden. I take Emmy up in my arms and throw her high up into the air. Jay and Rio embrace as do Miku and Ameana. We're so euphoric, Rio jokes that our happiness is going to kill him.

"We did it, baby!" Jay says, picking Emmy up. She laughs and hugs him back. By then, all of us are spread out in the garden, filled with a ridiculous amount of glee and energy. The sisters watch as we celebrate.

Emmy and I look at each other from across the garden. We don't need to use words. We know what the other is thinking and feeling.

We proved everyone wrong. We loved the way we wanted to and we never gave up. Everyone was wrong about us; our love didn't destroy us. It kept us alive…

We are so insane with excitement, we almost forget about the Amulet. But as promised, I hand it over to Chance and she thanks us.

"When will you be making your introduction to the Angel world?" Emmy asks.

"Soon. It's a delicate matter. We want to make sure it's the right time," Chance says.

"Well, good luck," Miku replies.

"We're sure you'll want to celebrate," Charity says to us.

"I'm so ready to party. Let's do this!" Jay announces.

"You're taken now. You have to ask Isabelle's permission to party," Ameana jokes.

"Wait, seriously?" he says, fear inhabiting his face.

All of us laugh mercilessly at Jay.

I pull Emmy against me and wrap my arms around her from behind, and together we look out onto the most beautiful thing we've ever seen: a world no longer in danger.

CHAPTER SIXTEEN: REPLAY

By the time we get back to New York City, every single angel on Earth has left us a Facebook message, text, or voice mail. That is if they weren't coming by our hotel in the plaza every five minutes. We've even had gift baskets filled with Snaps sent by the Original Paras.

In addition, angels visit us from every corner of the globe: London, Haiti, Japan, and Tibet. The Splash features all of us, including Emmy, Wolf, Tony, and Isabelle. It was front-page news:

"THEY ACTUALLY DID IT!!!

The Sage dropped by to congratulate us on a job very well done. He said how happy he was that things worked out differently than he saw it. He asked when we were planning on going back to the light.

"We can stay until midnight of the New Year, so in a few days," I tell him.

"Enjoy yourselves," he says kindly.

There's a party thrown in our honor just about every other day. I told the team that they could go to as many as they wanted. After all, work is over. We had found the map and eliminated every Akon. And Rage, if he survived the stabbing, would have his hands full with Lucy for failing to stop us.

Emmy wanted to join in the parties, but I made her go to Daraquin and get a full checkup. It took only a few hours to return her to perfect health. Even so, she was made to stay in bed by the Healers for a full two days.

So what does my girl want to do now that she is healed and rested? Go to a romantic city? Go on a shopping spree? See the pyramids?

No, Emmy wants to eat a gallon of rocky road ice cream on top of the Green Mountains. She dives into the container with gusto. I can't help but laugh at her.

"Hey, I have earned this! Don't you dare make fun of me," she warns.

"Your teeth are chattering."

"I do that so I can snuggle with you."

"You never need a reason to get next to me, you know that," I reply.

She moves closer and rests her head on my chest.

"Seriously, we should fly down from here."

She pays no attention to me. After she downs half the gallon, she pushes for us to do the other thing she came up here to do.

"This is crazy, Emmy. Christmas already passed," I protest.

"Well we were busy killing demons then, so we have to pretend like it hasn't passed. Please, Marcus!"

"I didn't bring your gift with me."

"But you said—"

"Okay, I *may* have remembered it." I smile.

"Yes!" she says, snuggling up to me.

"Sitting here on the edge of these mountains with you…this is the happiest I've been."

"Marcus Cane, don't you use sweet words to distract me. Where's my gift?" she says, bursting with excitement.

"Okay, okay. Here."

I hand her a small black box tied with a gold ribbon. I told her we angels don't celebrate human holidays but she insisted that I share it with her. The last time I cerebrated Christmas was back when I was human. I spent it with my family. I didn't know at the time it would be our last Christmas together.

"Now if you don't like it—" I start.

"I don't care if it's sand. I just like that you thought about me."

"I'm always thinking about you. You're hard to forget."

She kisses me and it feels like falling off the tallest mountain in the universe. It's exhilarating. It's intense. It's like being alive again.

Omnis, I will surrender all my lifetimes to have an extra day on Earth with her…

She pulls away from me gently and begins to unravel the ribbon. Watching her open the box, I suddenly start to miss the Christmases I won't get to share with her. Then I think about the birthdays and New Years I'll miss, too.

When you die those things stop mattering, but then I fell for a human, and now, they're all that matter…

"It's a Splash," she says, before she lifts the globe out from the box.

"It's not a Splash because it's not empty," I correct her.

She picks it up out of the box.

"It's a snow globe of a car in the snow."

"Whose car?" I ask her. She studies the orb closer.

"That's Jay's car. Wait! That's us inside the car!"

"It's called a Replay. It's like a snow globe, but it's alive. It's been constructed from memory. That memory is then played out by mini Shadow Servants made to look like the people in the memory."

"That's a mini Emmy and a mini Marcus inside Jay's car. And over there is my apartment building," she says, turning the grapefruit-sized orb in her hand.

"I had them reconstruct my favorite night: the night you kissed me."

She studies the Replay. The mini Shadow Servants interact and then kiss. The scene repeats itself as if on a loop.

"This is so crazy. It's even snowing like it was that night. The snow never stops falling. I don't even have to shake it. And they are wearing exactly what we were wearing that night!" She is completely taken with the Replay.

She runs her fingers over the dark wooden base of the orb. It has the date that she kissed me etched on it. I see her start to get weepy. The sight of her crying, even happy tears, really messes with my head. So I try to snap her out of it.

"I know I could have gotten you jewelry. I still can."

"Marcus, the most important thing you can give me is your Rah. I already have that."

"You really like the Replay?"

"I love it and I love you. Thank you so much."

She hugs me and whispers how happy she is.

"Okay, your turn," she says, handing me a red envelope. There is a handwritten message on the back.

"Let this bring you
what your love brought me:
Peace."

"What's in this?" I ask. She delights in the curiosity in my voice and tells me to open it. I tear into the envelope and find the most valuable thing I now own.

"Emmy, how did you…?"

I pull out a photograph of my parents and a little boy. They're smiling brightly with a Christmas tree in the background.

"That's Antony. Your little brother," she informs me. I can't stop looking at the picture even as I talk to her.

"Brother?"

"Yeah, he's a cutie."

"How did you get this?"

"I asked the twins, and they did their Tech magic and found out where your family lives now. And since you wouldn't let me out of your sight these past few weeks, Jay went to their house and took this from their mantel."

"My mom, she looks so…happy."

"She is. She has a blog about coping with the loss of a child. It gets a ton of traffic. Also, Jay found a certificate of completion from a rehab center on the wall."

"She's clean now?"

"She has been for a while now. Your death wasn't in vain."

I look at the picture again and fall silent.

"I know it probably brings up a lot of stuff, seeing them again."

"It does."

"Was the gift a bad idea?"

I look up at her.

"A bad idea? Emmy, this gift was… Thank you, baby."

I pull her close to me, wrap my arms around her, and kiss her fervently.

"When I lost my mom, I thought that was it. My world was gone. Just like that. But you took care of me, Marcus. You brought some of my world back to me. I just wanted to do the same for you."

"You did more than that. I can't believe in a few days, I'm never gonna see you again."

"Let's not talk about it. I can't take never seeing you again."

And so we laugh and talk as if there was no countdown to the New Year. As if I'm not about to go somewhere she isn't allowed to follow.

Like I said before, everyone wants to throw us a party. At one point, we had to turn a few angels down. But when we are given a party by *the* party girl herself, Arden, we simply can't refuse.

No one parties like the powerful Para. Her father is an Original. That comes with all kinds of serious obligations and duties. Her older sister is Rahell, the Taker. That is also a serious job. Every time an angel dies in battle, Rahell appears and takes his body to the house of fire. Rahell is the picture of dignity and restraint, while her sister, Arden, is…well, Arden.

She stands before me now in a sexy emerald futuristic-style dress. Her makeup is very much like her, striking and a little too much. But beyond the glitz and the glamour of Arden, she is a kind girl who's helped us out in the past.

"So, First Hottie, where is your human?" she asks.

"Since she is going to be alive for a few more decades, she decided to stay home and study."

"So she's a scholar?"

"Not really. I had to bribe her into it."

"What sinful act did you promise her?"

"I told her we'd be normal for one evening. We'd go to a movie and just hang. She's wanted that for a while now."

"Normal? Why would anyone aim for normal?" Arden laughs to herself. Then she holds up her drink and makes a toast to the crowd.

"Let the Coy flow and your inhibitions go!" she shouts.

Chapter Sixteen: Replay

The hundreds of angel partygoers can be heard screaming and cheering throughout every inch of the mansion. My team is more than happy to follow the partygoers' example.

Miku is dancing with the only guy who isn't scared of her or turned on by the fact that she used to be Redd. Jay and Isabelle talk over full glasses of Coy. Ameana is standing off to the side doing what I knew she'd be doing, pretending not to stand next to Wolf (while standing next to Wolf). He's fully recovered thanks to the Healers at Daraquin.

The only Guardian I don't see is Rio. I call his cell and it goes straight to voice mail. I head off towards the unlikely couple. They're deep in conversation but it's hard to tell if it's a personal one or not.

"So, is there any other member of your team you kissed?" Wolf asks.

Okay, definitely personal. And for Wolf, very dangerous.

"I don't owe you a rundown of who I have and have not been with," my ex counters.

"I just need to know how many angels I have to compete against to get you."

"I'm not a prize," she says.

"So far…no," Wolf mumbles.

"What is your problem?"

"You work hand in hand with your ex. I'm about free love but that's too free."

"Why does it matter to you who I work with?"

"You know why."

"Wolf, I can't be what you need, okay?"

"Why?"

"Because I'm not into that anymore."

"Oh, so you're into girls?"

"Funny."

"I know a lot of really cool lesbian angels. I could introduce you."

"I meant I'm done with dating."

"Forever?"

"Yeah."

"Your aura is getting dark. That's what happens when you lie."

"I'm not lying. I'm done with relationships."

"Well, then it's too bad because you're already in one."

"I told you before, you and I—"

"I mean you and Marcus."

"He walked out of our relationship months ago."

"Exactly," he says. She looks at him, confused. He turns to her and closes the gap between them.

"Ameana, Marcus left you months ago, but you're still standing here having a relationship with his ghost. Marcus walked away, why can't you?"

Not wanting to hear the answer, I clear my throat loudly.

"Hey, I'm sorry to interrupt but have you guys seen Rio?" I ask.

"He said he was going back to the house," Wolf replies. Ameana is avoiding eye contact with both of us.

"Okay, thanks," I say awkwardly.

I know the mission is over, but since we lost Reese, I don't like not knowing where my team is. So I head back to the house. Once there, I head to Rio's room and find it empty.

I call his cell and it goes to voice mail. I turn on the tracker that the council gave us months ago. Most of the time it is accurate about our location but we stopped using it because it wasn't one hundred percent. I call Jay to see if he might know where Rio is.

"No, I haven't seen him. Did you ask the other Wonder Twin?"

"I don't want to worry her if he's just talking a walk or something."

"Yeah, you're right. Do you need me to help you find him?"

"No, it's okay. Stay and hang out with Isabelle. Just watch the others for me."

"No problem. Hey, is it cool if I mention the Quo to Isabelle? I mean they should be a hot topic soon, right?" he asks.

"We did promise to keep it quiet but they should be out in the open in a few days so…yeah, I guess."

I hang up with Jay and call Emmy, but she hasn't seen Rio.

"Have you tried his cell?" she asks.

"All I get is voice mail."

"Marcus, relax, everyone is just blowing off steam. You should be, too. Weren't you supposed to be at Arden's party?"

"Yeah but—"

"But you went all First Guardian and overprotective. The mission is complete. When will you give yourself a break?"

"You're right. I can hang back for about an hour. If I don't hear from him by then, I'll gather the team."

"Sounds reasonable. Now, go and party."

"If you're done with studying, maybe you can come with?"

"Actually, I am done studying. But I have company."

"Who?"

"Okay, don't read too much into this, but it's Julian."

"Really?"

"Yeah, we've been talking about what my mom was like on the bridge. And I've been telling him stories about her that I haven't really let myself remember until now. It was too painful, ya know?"

"Yeah, I do…"

"But you can come over if you want."

"No, you two keep talking."

"Okay, but remember—tomorrow, you, me, normal."

"Got it."

I stay at the house and Rio returns an hour later.

"I was about to send a search party. Where were you?" I ask.

"Flying around."

"Flying around where?"

"Um… I don't know, Mom."

"Look, I'm not trying to be a jerk but I was calling you all night."

"What happened? Is Miku okay?"

"She's fine. Everyone is fine."

"Then what's the problem?"

"I just like knowing where everyone is."

"Look, I know I'm always getting on you about stuff, but in the end, you did a great job. We saved the world and have time to celebrate. You did it."

"More of a team effort kind of thing."

"Yeah, but you made sure we held it together. You can relax, First Guardian. The battle is over. We have won."

The battle is finally over. And yeah, we won…

CHAPTER SEVENTEEN: THE QUESTION

It was a total waste of human money for Emmy and I to go to the movies. We never watched the screen. We took turns staring at each other. And when we weren't doing that, we were kissing or laughing at nothing in particular. At some point in the movie, the guy tells the girl he's going to have to save the world from a nuclear reaction plant.

"We saved the world and they didn't put us in a fancy movie," Emmy whispers.

"Yeah, but it took us a year. This guy saves the world in an hour and a half," I remark.

She beams at me and I take her hand. I tell her it's time to bail out of the movie. Emmy agrees. We head out of the movie theater. Once outside we're surrounded by the bright lights of Times Square.

"I'm hungry," she announces.

"We could get anything you want, anywhere in the world."

"Hot dog from that guy," she says, pointing to the hot dog vendor a few feet away.

"That's all you want?"

"Yeah."

"You're a cheap date."

"Not so fast, First Guardian. I also want a pretzel and drink."

"That's a lot of money."

"A girl's gotta eat."

We head to the hot dog cart, where my girl puts away three hot dogs, two pretzels, and soda. I look at her with total astonishment.

"What? My appetite's back."

"You ate enough for four people."

Chapter Seventeen: The Question

She laughs and wipes her mouth. I shake my head and marvel at how easy it is to make her happy.

"So what do you want to do after our fine dining experience?" she asks.

"I was thinking we could have another experience," I say, taking her hand in mine.

I pull her close to me and press my lips against hers. It still amazes me that anyone can feel this good. Kissing her always causes my wings to flutter uncontrollably. Her eyes are closed, so she doesn't notice just how much her touch affects me. It's crazy; I should be able to kiss this girl and not completely lose control.

"I was thinking we could go to Bangkok, they have a hotel there with a spectacular view. Or maybe we could go to the mountains. Or maybe—"

"Marcus. Slow down."

I laugh at the thought of *Emmy* telling me to slow down.

"Sorry, look if you're not ready, you know that's fine with me. In fact, it's great. I mean I don't really need to…I mean we don't have to…I mean—"

I sound like a complete idiot.

"Marcus. I want to make love to you and I want it to be tonight. I was just thinking it would be nice to be together where I spent the most time thinking about us—my room. Is that okay?"

"As long as I get to be with you, yeah."

"Can you give me a few minutes before you come over? I want to freshen up," she says.

We head down an alley. I throw out a Port and she hops onto it.

"I will see you in a half hour," she vows with a quick kiss.

She disappears and I decide to walk to her place. By the time I get there she should be ready. I've played this moment over and over again in my mind. The thought of finally being with her causes my wings to go crazy, seriously.

Marcus, be cool. Just remember she's human and don't let the light from your soul overwhelm her. The first time she has sex shouldn't be the last time.

I try to maintain my cool and just think of it as any other night, but it's just not working. The thought that I will finally be able to hold her and be with her for the entire night overwhelms me with anticipation. That's when I realize I'm not walking, I'm flying.

Damn…

I don't even know when I took to the air. It doesn't matter. I told her I would give her some time to herself and that's what I'm gonna do. So I stand across the street from her building. I have a perfect view of her bedroom window. As she gets ready, she puts on a playlist. I can hear her music floating in the air.

She's playing "Staying Alive." It's her favorite song to be silly with. The best part about it is she will eventually give in to the emotion of the music and start dancing. She dances this awful '70s disco dance that should be outlawed. I remember the first time I caught her dancing to it. We had been in a huge argument and she wasn't talking to me. Miku made me go and invite her to dinner so we could learn more about her.

I walked into her apartment and found her dancing to "Staying Alive." I never told her but that was the moment I knew I loved her. When we first met, I knew I wanted her but that's different than love. Standing there watching her outdated, heartfelt moves, I knew in my soul I was in love with Emerson Hope Baxter.

Okay, that's enough time. I've watched her come out of the shower with a towel on, change outfits four times, and thank the city of Detroit for attending her "concert." Finally it's time to be with the girl I love.

Thank you, Omnis…

I make myself take a moment and reduce the flapping of my wings to that of a normal angel. Then I head across the street to where "my everything" awaits me.

"Off to have sex with my child, Marcus?"

Oh, you have got to be freaking kidding me!

I turn and find Julian behind me.

"What are you doing here?" I ask, working really hard not to lose my temper.

"So you're really gonna do it?"

"This isn't your business."

"Like hell. That's my kid."

"Look, I'm not doing this with you, okay? If you can't tell how much I love your daughter by now then you just don't get it."

"I know you love her."

"Then what's your problem? If Emmy didn't want us to be together tonight she would have said something. Your daughter isn't shy. She says what's on her mind."

"You think this is about the two of you having sex?"

"Isn't it?"

"No, it's not."

"Fine, then. What the hell is this about?"

"You have loved and protected Emmy every single step of the way in this mission. I respect that."

"Okay…"

"When you went to Difi and set her forest on fire, Lucy retaliated by ripping Femi's heart out. Now Emmy and the rest of your team has killed her son."

"What's your point?"

"The Guardians go back into the light in a few days. You will not be permitted back on Earth. What happens when Lucy wants revenge and you're gone? Who do you think she'll go after?"

A chill runs through my entire body as I face the window where Emmy is now playing with Ms. Charlotte. It never once occurred to me that Lucy would go after her. How could I be so stupid? How could I have missed that?

Julian, seeing me in deep thought, puts his hand on my shoulder.

"Marcus, I was wrong before. You do love her. It's that love that's blinding you from reality. It did the same to me. But unlike me, you have a chance to save Emmy."

"I could have angels around her twenty-four seven."

"The council won't allow you to use their resources like that."

"I could have her placed in some kind of a Holder."

"For the rest of her life?"

"Everyone knows we have to go back into the light. So Emmy and I are over no matter what."

"It doesn't matter. As long as she means something to you, she's not safe."

"Julian, what do I do?"

"Emmy will always be a target because by getting to her, they can get to you."

"You want me to break up with her?"

"No, it wouldn't work. She'd never believe all of a sudden you just don't love her."

"You're right. She'd never buy it. Damn it!" I shout, smashing my foot through the headlights of the nearest parked car.

Julian is in deep thought. Suddenly, he looks up at me as if a light bulb has gone off in his head.

"Marcus, you have to make her worst fear come to life."

"Which is?"

"You and Ameana."

"What?"

"You have to get back with your ex. It's the only thing you can do to secure Emmy's future."

I can actually feel the happiness being drained from me. My getting back with Ameana would crush Emmy, but it's also the best way to convince evil that Emmy no longer means anything to me.

"Julian, I can't…"

He tells me how sorry he is that things have to be that way. I can barely make out what he's saying. My only focus now is the beautiful girl in the window waiting for me.

Julian walks off and leaves me standing in the same spot: across the street from the only girl I love. I should have been at her door half an hour ago. It's only a matter of time before she calls me and asks why I'm late.

I think maybe I should chance it. Maybe Lucy won't come after her. In that moment, I am blissful. In that moment, I run across the street and hold her. We spend a night sharing our passions, secrets and, dreams. She runs her fingers through my wings and her touch brings with it a state of pleasure so pure, it moves the heavens.

Then I think: what if Lucy does go after her? Lucy has lost the map in other Cycles but this is the first one where the clue is a human. Julian's right; it's not in the nature of evil to forgive. There's no telling what she would do to Emmy. To make matters worse, I keep hearing Julian's voice in my head:

"What happens when you're gone?"

That question is the reason why I don't run over to see her. That question is the reason why I don't pick up my cell when it rings, and the reason I'm about to cruelly push away everything I've ever wanted.

"Are you busy?" I ask awkwardly, standing in the doorway of her room. She turns and faces me.

"What is it?"

"I was wondering if we could talk."

"I guess."

I enter Ameana's room and close the door behind me.

"Whatever he's about to ask, it's really important to him, so make him suffer," Rio shouts from his room.

"Stop reading my Wave and mind your business," I shout back. Ameana smiles despite herself.

"Could I get rich off this favor you're about to ask? If so, we may have to stop off in Paris before we go back to the light."

"You can't take these clothes with you. You'd only wear them for a few days."

"A few minutes in couture will satisfy a girl for a lifetime," she informs me.

I laugh at her. She smiles back at me. She hasn't done that in months. For a few moments I replay what we were like in the beginning. Ameana and I were opposites that complemented each other. Then over time we just became…opposites.

Still, there is nothing on Earth or in the light more radiant than Ameana Jones. Her smile illuminates every room she enters. I always wished she'd smile more. But even stone cold serious, there's an effortless grace in the way she does just about everything.

"I need to ask you for a favor." I hear the words coming out of my mouth yet I still can't believe what I'm about to ask.

"What's the favor?"

"I realized even without the Triplex, evil will always be on the hunt for Emmy."

"Well, evil has never been good at losing so…yeah."

"The only way I can guarantee that evil doesn't come after her is to make everyone believe she no longer matters to me. That way they won't hurt her in retaliation."

"Okay…" she says, not sure where the conversation is headed.

"In order to do that, we have to break up." The words are so heavy they drop to the center of the room.

"What does this have to do with me?" she asks.

"Knowing Emmy, she'd see past whatever it is I say. She'd know that I was breaking up with her to protect her. At this point my words wouldn't be enough. She would need to see proof that I no longer love her."

"Marcus, what are you asking?"

"I need you to pretend to get back together with me."

"Unbelievable," she says, clearly pissed.

"I know it's crazy, but it's the only way Emmy will buy that I suddenly don't want her anymore. We're only here for a few more days. It's not like I could fall in love with another girl in that time. The only thing she'd buy is that I went back to you."

"That's crazy."

"Ameana, this is the only way to save her from danger in the future."

"I'm going to say this slowly so that you understand each and every word that comes out of my mouth. I. Don't. Give. A. Damn. About. Emmy."

"What about me? Do you still care about me?"

"How dare you try and use my feelings for you. You're such an ass!"

"I know I have no right to ask this. If there was any other way…"

"No, Marcus. I'm not getting back with you to save your girlfriend. I think I've given up more than enough to Emmy and you."

"You're right. You shouldn't have to do this. But I'm hoping you will anyway."

"Why? Are you going to order me to pretend to get back with you?"

"No."

"Good, then we're done here," she says, turning her back to me. As I reach for the doorknob, I turn around and address her one last time:

"When we're gone, Lucy could take her easily. She could be on her way to school, in her bed sleeping. Suddenly, she's being set on fire or ripped apart limb by limb or drowning in a pool of her own blood in some alley. Why? Because she loved the wrong guy."

"Marcus, what you're asking me to do crosses the line."

"I love her, Ameana. There are no lines."

"I'm sorry, Marcus."

I nod slightly and close the door behind me.

Now in the living room, I think back to when I first met her. She had her hair in a messy ponytail and wore an ill-fitted "Piglet" T-shirt. I was cold and rude to her, all the while wanting to spend the rest of my days looking into her eyes.

The thought of her dying on Earth alone causes a sharp pain to run across my chest. I can't stop the images from coming to me. I see her in my head, broken, bloody, and still.

"Okay, I'll do it," Ameana says behind me. I turn and find her standing in the living room, looking unhappy but settled.

"Really?" I ask.

"I'll pretend to get back with you."

I run up to her and embrace her tightly. Had she been human I would definitely have injured her. She pulls away.

"Don't do that," she says softly. She reads the confusion on my face. "This is just pretend. I need you to remember that."

"Yeah, of course."

"Good." She clears her throat.

"Thank you so much."

"Whatever," she says, unable to look me in the eye.

"I don't want to mess this arrangement up, but I think you should talk to Wolf."

"We're not going out."

I roll my eyes.

"Well, your 'not' boyfriend will want to know anyway."

I discuss the plan with the rest of the team. While they think it's cruel to betray Emmy, they understand that it is in her best interest.

"Rio, she's gonna come to you and ask if I am hiding something."

"You want me to lie?"

"It's for her own good."

"Yeah, I guess."

"I need you guys to find I.M. Trouble and have him write about Ameana and I being back together. It needs to be front page of the Splash. That way everyone will know."

"Yeah, I'm on it," Jay assures me.

The team must feel my apprehension because they begin to reassure me.

"It's what has to be done," Jay says.

"Emmy deserves a normal life after everything that's happened. You're giving that to her. That's a good thing," Miku adds.

"The worst part is what I have to do next…" I tell them my plan.

"You're really going to do that?" Rio says.

"Yeah, she'll hate me but that way we can sell the story better."

"How will you feel about her hating you?" Miku asks.

"It's fine," I lie. No one buys it.

"Did Ameana tell Wolf her plans yet?" Jay asks.

"She's on the roof talking to him right now."

As soon as I say the words, we hear a very irate rocker angel shouting from the rooftop.

"WHAT??? THAT'S SO NOT RIGHTEOUS!!!"

We head up to the roof. I'm not sure if we go up to make sure Ameana is okay or if we just want to spy. Judging by the way we are all careful not to interrupt them, I'm thinking we are spying more than anything.

The two of them are on the other side of the roof. They're too deep in conversation to realize, or care, that we are there. Wolf is pacing back and forth as his wings rage against the sky.

"This isn't about me and Marcus," she insists.

"Everything you do is about Marcus," he protests.

"Look, I know it's a strange situation but—"

"Pretending to get back with your ex, who you aren't over, is not strange. It's stupid."

"I'm over Marcus."

"Please, you walk around like an open wound."

"Wolf, I'm trying very hard not to throw you off the roof. Help me by not being such a pain."

"Me? Because of you, all my chakras are out of line!"

"Well, put them back in line and control yourself. I told you we're only pretending."

"See, okay. There goes my yin. And wait, yeah. There goes my yang. Now both yin and yang—unbalanced."

"You're doing it to yourself."

"No, you're doing it to me. This whole time, all I have wanted is you. And now I see you don't want me. You want Marcus. You will always want Marcus."

"That's not true! Not anymore."

"Really? How the hell am I supposed to know you want me? Huh? You act like we aren't together. You won't let me save your life. You won't even return my calls. How am I supposed to know—"

Ameana shuts him up by wrapping her arms around his shoulders and giving him a big, long, deep kiss.

The team cheers and makes crude remarks.

"It's about damn time," Jay says.

"How's your yin and yang now?" Rio asks.

"Leave some for me," Miku yells out to her best friend.

Wolf picks his angel up and flies away with her, never once breaking from the kiss.

CHAPTER EIGHTEEN: THE ANOMALY

The next morning, I find Emmy has called me several times. I call her back and brace myself.

"Hey."

"Marcus! Where were you? I was gonna come find you but Ben's mom needed me to babysit at the last minute. Is everything okay?" she asks frantically.

No, I'm about to break your heart and in turn break mine. And I would fight Lucy all over again if it meant that I didn't have to do what I'm about to do.

"Yeah, I'm good."

"Why didn't you come over?"

"Something came up."

"Is the team okay?"

"Yeah, it's just some stuff I had to take care of."

"You sound weird. Are you sure you're okay?"

"Yeah…"

"I'm coming over."

"No, everything's fine. Don't come over, okay? I'll see you later."

"But—"

"Please, Emmy. Don't come."

I hang up before she can protest more. Rio comes up to the roof and stands alongside me.

"You told her not to come?" he asks.

"The only way I can get her here is to tell her to stay away," I reply.

"Guess you have it all figured out."

"Yeah, I'm a freaking genius," I spit out bitterly.

Chapter Eighteen: The Anomaly

I head to my room, where Ameana is waiting. She was able to get Wolf to agree to the plan. The two of them are going to be low-key until we get into the light. It's been a few hours since she and Wolf became unofficially "official." Strands of her hair are glowing.

"Wow, that good, huh?" I ask her.

"What are you talking about?" she says, playing coy.

"I'm glad you have someone. He's different but he's a good guy."

"That doesn't mean it will end well."

"Doesn't mean it won't."

"He wants me to take yoga."

I burst out laughing and she playfully pushes me away.

"Can I get pictures of that?" I ask.

"I don't think so."

"Wolf has no idea what he's in for."

"Everyone thinks I'm a handful, but what about the angel who stops in the middle of an argument to find his chakra?"

The more she talks, the harder I laugh.

She looks out the window and tells me Emmy is on her way upstairs.

"Okay."

"You sure about this?" she asks.

I can't bring myself to talk. I can only clear my throat and nod.

Ameana goes over to the door and leaves it slightly ajar.

We hear Emmy's footsteps as she makes her way up the stairs. Even though I know this has to happen, a very real part of me hopes she can see through this scheme. I hope she knows that I love her even with what I'm about to do.

I hear her call out my name as she heads down the hallway towards us. I pull Ameana close. Emmy opens the door. She finds me and Ameana in the middle of an all-consuming kiss.

Her jaw drops. Her body shakes uncontrollably. She gasps as if someone is ripping the very breath from her lungs. The tears spring to her eyes like a tidal wave of pain.

She's trying to make sense of the picture before her. But no matter how she puts the pieces together, the picture is still the same. She lets out a whimper like a kitten who's just been brutally kicked. She looks at me, silently begging for an explanation.

"I'm sorry" are the only words I can choke out.

She runs out the door. I follow her. She heads to the roof, I'm right behind her.

"Why?" she pleads.

"I don't know why."

"TELL ME WHY!" she screams as she shakes with rage and confusion.

"I thought I stopped loving her, but I was wrong," I lie.

"You love her?"

"Yes."

"You don't love me anymore?"

"No."

"Did you ever love me?"

"I thought I did in the beginning."

"And now?"

"No, I don't love you."

She gasps for air, she can't breathe. I run over to her and take her hand. She violently brushes my hand away.

"DON'T TOUCH ME!!!"

"I'm sorry. I should have told you I still had feelings for her. I thought they would stop eventually."

"Go away," she whispers.

"Emmy. I'm—"

"GO AWAY! I HATE YOU! I HATE YOU! I HATE YOU!" she shrieks loudly as she pounds her fists into my chest.

I fight the desire to take her into my arms and hold her. Then I force myself to do the impossible: I walk away from the only person who has made me feel alive since my death.

I look over my shoulder and see her crumple onto the floor of the roof. Her sobbing causes her small frame to rock back and forth. I think about going back to her and telling her the truth.

This is for her, Marcus. Walk away because you love her. She deserves better than being hunted all her life...

Chapter Eighteen: The Anomaly

As I open the door to go downstairs, an unnatural darkness takes over the once blue sky. Somehow I know what is happening even before I feel it on my skin.

The blue raindrops hit the palm of my hand. I look up and all of New York City is bathed in blue rain. For the first time in the history of man and angel kind, a human has drained the blue from the sky.

I didn't just break Emmy's heart; I took what was left of her world…

I should have gone to the Green Mountains. I should have left Earth entirely but I couldn't. I had to stay and make sure the whole Angel world knew that Ameana and I were back together. The truth is what angels know, demons know. And I need every demon to know and report back to Lucy that Emmy and I are done. That way she will finally get some much needed peace.

There's another reason why I don't leave New York City: I need to look in on her. The others said they would do it for me, but it's not the same thing. I needed to see with my own eyes that she's okay. And of course, she isn't.

I swallow "No See" Snaps so I can be invisible and look in on her. It pains me to see her and know what I've done. So why can't I stay away? Why am I glued to the one place that causes me so much anguish?

It's been two days since the blue rain. Every human is talking about the day it rained a color. Scientists from all points of the globe have descended on New York City to study what they call "an anomaly." Even angels are fascinated by it. Although they now know the story of Isis and Demetri was a true, it's still an amazing sight to behold in their lifetime.

Luckily it only lasted a few hours. Had Emmy caused it to rain longer, I'm not sure what we could have done to make the rain stop. I don't want her to suffer the same fate as Isis. The Sage admits even he didn't know a human could make that happen. But then again, Emmy isn't like any other human I know.

The Splash talked about the blue rain but that was after they spent several pages talking about Ameana and I reuniting. We have made the front page of the Splash. I suspect we will be there for some time.

I only know about it because Emmy is reading the Splash in bed. She has reread the article at least ten times. After she reads it, she looks at the Replay I gave her. She watches it for hours. She then curls up in her comforter and cries. It's the most heart-wrenching sound I've ever heard a human make. I sit at the foot of her bed and watch over her.

She cries for hours on end. And when she has exhausted herself, she feeds Ms. Charlotte and drifts off to sleep. I've taken a lot of Snaps in order to be able to watch her. The team says I need to rest. I don't care about recharging. I'm gonna stay with my love until the council forces us to come back to the light.

A few days later, sitting by her bed like I normally do, something strange happens. When it's time to feed Ms. Charlotte, she doesn't get up. She just stays there staring off into space. The cat meows over and over again and she doesn't respond.

I call Rio and he confirms what I feared, Emmy is severely depressed. It was better when she was crying because then she was feeling something. But now it's like she's numb and doesn't care about anything.

I remember how she was when she lost Sara. She was almost catatonic. I can't let her go through that again. But then Rio reminds me that there is nothing I can do to help her. I spend every waking moment by her side just like before only now, she never moves. She doesn't cry. She doesn't do anything.

So now when Ms. Charlotte cries, I feed her. I have the grocery store deliver food although I know Emmy won't eat. She looks pale and weak so I buy her vitamins, even though I'm sure she won't take them. I've taken to straightening up her apartment when she's asleep.

Jay enters the apartment and observes me with a sense of wonder.

"What is it?" I ask.

"I'ma be real with you, I've seen you put your life in danger for Emmy many times. But I have never seen a guy, angel or human, dust his girl's apartment. That's love, man."

"She's not my girl anymore," I lament.

"She know you come in here and do this?"

"No, when she's awake, I take a Snap and disappear."

"Words out everywhere: You and Ameana are back together."

"Good."

"Wolf hates you."

"I get that."

"And Rio's been staying away from this place."

"Emmy's emotions are that strong?"

"Marcus, she *made* it rain blue. This from a girl with no powers."

"Where's Rio?"

"Since the rain, he's been on the other side of the world. You know how it is for him when someone feels only one thing. He feels the full extent of that. Sometimes it's more than he can handle. Only way he could function is to get some distance. Emmy's pain is so concentrated—"

"I know about her pain, Jay."

"My bad," he says, walking off.

I text Miku and tell her to take credit should Emmy ask who did it. Miku tells me I should stay away. She says it's unhealthy for me to watch Emmy suffer. She thinks it's a way of torturing myself. I don't know if she's right or not. I'm not sure it matters. I'm not sure anything matters really.

Days later, after feeding Ms. Charlotte, I walk into the room, invisible as usual, and find Emmy on the phone. It's only now I realize how much I miss hearing her voice. Does this mean she's okay now?

Are you okay after only a few days? I ask myself. But this is different. Emmy is strong. In many ways, she's stronger than me. She just doesn't know it. I listen carefully to her conversation.

"No, not later. I need to see you now. Please, Rio?"

She waits for his response.

"Great. Thank you!" She puts the phone down and bites her lip. I know what she wants to ask him. She's about to be hurt yet again.

Damn…

Half an hour later, Rio comes over to Emmy's apartment. He knows I'm there because he reads my Waves in the room.

"I'm thinking maybe Marcus is under some kind of spell. Ya know like something someone found at the market?"

"He's not," Rio says gently.

"How do you know?"

"The market doesn't really deal with matters of love."

"Oh. Maybe he's just afraid because we won't be able to spend more than a day together. And maybe he doesn't want me to be alone."

"That's not it."

"Then what is it?"

"He loves Ameana."

"Are you sure? Are you absolutely sure?"

"Yes. I'm sorry."

"Does he have any feelings for me?"

"He cares about you—a lot."

"You know what I mean."

"No, he doesn't love you anymore."

"Thank you for being honest with me, Rio."

Rio takes her hand and sits beside her in bed.

"How are you?" he asks her.

"Don't you know already?"

"Yeah. But it's rude not to ask."

"I'm okay. You guys are sweet to bring me food and stuff. Thank you."

He raises an eyebrow but doesn't say anything.

"I feel so…unwanted."

"You're not unwanted. We love you. You know what an unbelievably great person you are, right? You helped save billions of lives."

"Yeah."

"C'mon, let me take you out."

"Another time," she says, as she crawls back into bed.

Rio heads out the door. I appear before him in the hallway.

"Marcus, it's not fair to her. Let the girl grieve in peace," Rio insists.

"I just want her to be okay."

"Well, that's not gonna happen. You broke her heart. I know the reasons you did it. That doesn't change the fact that she has to go through this. Give the girl some privacy. Damn."

Chapter Eighteen: The Anomaly

Rio doesn't usually get pissed off. I guess he sees something in her Wave that tells him she really needs to be alone. I nod and take off to the Green Mountains.

Once there, I sit on the highest peak and look down at the world below.

"Angels make horrible suicide jumpers," Jay says.

"Who told you I was here?"

"Rio."

Jay sits beside me.

"You remember the last time we were here? You were beef'n with Ameana?" he offers.

"Yeah. Guess I always sucked in relationships."

"Well, you ain't got skillz like the kid," he brags.

"I destroyed her."

"You know what I learned about Emmy? Never ever count that girl out."

"That's true."

"She survived the Akons and Lucy. I think she'll survive being in love."

"At least one of us will," I joke.

"C'mon, let's go play some Runner Ball. We leave Earth in a few hours. We should get some play time in. After that, we need to talk about the Triplets."

"What about them?"

"Well, I was wondering why—you know what? Screw it. Let's go play some ball."

I reluctantly agree and the two of us fly back to the hotel to see if the others want to join in. We round up the rest of the Guardians. Suddenly the thought of playing Runner Ball excites me. I need something, anything to shake the misery of the past few days.

As we gather in the living room of the deluxe suite, there is a knock on the door. Miku goes to answer it. When she comes up the stairs, Emmy is behind her.

"Hi guys," she says. Her voice is soft and slightly hoarse.

Everyone greets her except Ameana. Emmy turns her attention towards me.

"I was gonna check on you but I thought you needed space," I say, sounding way too eager.

"No need to check up on me."

"Yeah I know, I just…I'm glad you're okay. Look if you want to talk…"

"I don't need to talk. I just needed to stop off and give you this."

She hands me a glass casing with red liquid inside it.

"You're giving me my Rah back?"

"Yes. You'll need it for…"

"Wait. You don't have to give it back to me right now."

"Yeah, I do…"

She extends her hand once again. I take it from her. She heads out the door.

"Emmy…" I call out to her desperately.

She stops but doesn't turn around. She simply says the words I've dreaded hearing since I first laid eyes on her.

"Goodbye, Marcus."

CHAPTER NINETEEN: GOING HOME

It's our last day on Earth. There's sadness in the air. I don't think any of us thought we'd come to miss humans or Earth itself. We just assumed we'd save the world and never look back. We were wrong about that. In fact, we were wrong about a lot of things.

I allow everyone to spend their last day anyway they want to. Rio is off traveling somewhere on the other side of the world. Jay and Isabelle will continue to see each other in the light so leaving isn't as difficult for him, although I know he's gotten very close to Emmy and he hates to say goodbye to her.

Miku and Ameana are off giving their designer clothes to Goodwill and other charities. Jay had to give Siren away. If he could cry, I think he would have. The only saving grace was that he was able to give it away to a family desperately in need of money.

They all call to check up on me throughout the day. They ask if I need company. I tell them I'm okay. They are nice enough to pretend to believe me. And even if I was to be honest with them, what could they do for me? What can anyone do for me?

They ask where I am and I tell them I'm playing Runner Ball with a few Ground Walkers. Rio, being Rio, knows I'm lying but that's the great thing about him, he acts like he can't read your Wave sometimes.

So, where am I?

I have no idea. I'm surrounded by mountains from every angle. I can't even remember how it is I got here. I've been lost in thought ever since she came over…

I thought no matter what happened I would be spending my last day on Earth near her. I could take "No See" Snaps and be with her all day. But it turns out there is a limit to how much pain a First Guardian can take.

I didn't reach my breaking point with Hun, Rage, or Kairo. The one that broke me weighs about a hundred and fifteen pounds, has no powers, and can't fly. Yet she was able to bring me to a place of total despair.

I can't stand to be in the same hemisphere she is. Let alone the same room. I can't stand to be around her beautiful eyes, soft lips, and enduring smile. I know I hurt her beyond reason, I just didn't think she'd give me my Rah back. Why didn't she fight for us like Ameana did?

Because you betrayed her, embarrassed her, and broke her heart, and all she did was love you unconditionally.

I tell myself that we would have parted anyway but it does little to ease my mind. We knew it would end eventually but we were supposed to have the last few days. We were supposed to be together until the final seconds before midnight.

There's a question she asked a while back. It's a question I'm asking myself now: Do I have any regrets? If I could go back to that moment in the living room when I first saw her—messy hair, cartoon T-shirt and all, would I change anything?

If I could somehow make it so that none of it ever happened, would I? If I knew this kind of devastation was possible when love doesn't work, would I still have fallen?

Yes. Idiot.

I know very well what my answer is. But I don't understand why it's that way. Who walks into a situation knowing the end would be so brutal?

I'd only do it for her…

She's the only girl who could have driven me to the lengths I have gone to. I look back and try to find mistakes that I've made, moments where I could have been wiser, points in time where I could have said "let's not fall in love."

But instead of finding moments that I would change, my mind finds moments that I want to hold on to. I seek them out and replay them like a playlist on eternal repeat.

When she first said my name…

Chapter Nineteen: Going Home

How adorable she was when she came to dinner and worried the team would disappear into their memories and never come back…

The way she can confront demons like Kairo, but hides her eyes during scary movies…

The way her skin feels beneath my fingers…

The moment she sees I'm losing hope, she lets herself get thrown into a dumpster so I'll laugh…

Oh yeah, her laugh…

The way she holds tight to hope no matter what…

The books that she's read a million times but keeps nearby so she can read them a million more…

Her kiss…

Her body against mine…

The way she loves… I will never again be loved the way she loved me. And that, that is the pain I will not recover from.

The moment she stopped loving me is the moment I died, again.

I take my Rah out of my pocket and study it. It's something I didn't think I would ever have again after I laid eyes on her. Now it's in my hand. No one wants it. No one is asking for it. And even if they did, they can't have my Rah.

It belongs to her. It will always belong to her…

I spot an opening on the mountainside. I walk in and look around. Here seems as good a place as any. I carefully make a small hole in the side of the mountain and insert my Rah.

I always envisioned her and I doing this together…

I can't see a world where I don't hurt anymore. I wish I was human. Humans live eighty or ninety years, then their pain is gone. I will live thousands of years with a gaping wound that her love once filled.

I spend a few hours in the mountains trying not to think about her. I fail as I expected I would. Finally I push myself off the mountain and fly back to New York City. I can't even fly over her neighborhood without missing her.

Damn, there's got to be a mixture to make this hurt go away.

I head over to see if Miku and Ameana need help giving their massive piles of clothes away. I need to focus on something else, anything.

As I walk the cold New York streets, I run into happy partygoers. They are all rushing off to Times Square to see the ball drop in a few hours. The streets are flooded with happy couples, families, and friends. The mood is upbeat despite the bitter cold.

I wonder what she's doing right now…

My cell rings just in time to keep me from a dangerous train of thought. I'm grateful to whoever is calling on the other line. I see it's Jay and wonder what he's come up with to keep me distracted.

"You don't have to keep calling to check on me, I'm good," I tell him.

"Hey, there's something I think you need to see," Jay says, sounding far more serious than I have heard him in the past few days.

"What is it?"

"We may be wrong."

"Who is we?"

"Me and Isabelle."

"Wrong about what?"

"We're at her family's house. She has a huge collection of history books."

"Okay…"

"Well, I told her about the Quo and she thinks she's read about them before."

"They said they have never been out into the Angel world."

"Then why is there a chapter dedicated to them in the Tri-history, volume three?"

"Are you sure it's about them?"

"It doesn't say 'Quo' but it talks about angels mingling with humans."

"Okay, so a few people may know about them, so what?"

"According to this book, they've been around for many Cycles and the council kept them at bay because they were afraid."

"Yeah, they were afraid it would mess up the balance."

"No, Marcus, the council was afraid. Like actual fear."

"Why would they fear the Quo?"

"I don't know."

"Okay, I'll take a look at the book but let's do it after we get to the light."

"Okay."

"You and Isabelle meet us at the take off point."

"Done."

The take off point is near a small village in West Africa. It shouldn't take long to get there, so while we still have some time, I head to see if the girls need my help.

There's another reason why I want to see the girls. I'm sure Ameana didn't go to see Emmy but Miku would certainly say goodbye to her before she goes. A part of me is hoping that Miku will tell me she asked about me.

That is so pathetic…

I see the girls heading out of Goodwill but Miku goes back towards the hotel and Ameana walks in the opposite direction. Maybe she's meeting Wolf. She checks to see if she's being followed, then double-checks again.

Why is she acting so suspicious? At this point everyone knows that her and Wolf are together. Though I'm sure she didn't mention to him that Rage saved her life.

I follow her as she dodges into an alley a few streets over. She takes off into the sky. I follow at a safe distance. Something tells me she could be in danger. I have learned to follow my instincts as leader over the past few months.

Well, on anything but love…

She flies to the West Coast, to an out-of-the-way beach with a hidden cave. She double-checks to make sure she's alone. I quickly pull back.

What is she doing here?

Maybe this is some romantic tryst she and Wolf are having before they go into the light. I think about maybe turning back and giving them their privacy. But again, something tells me to stay with her. She walks into the cave toward a figure I can't make out.

There's a fire burning in the center. It gives everything a warm orange glow. The flames enable me to make out a shadow along the wall. Ameana is in the cave with a male figure who has wings.

So, I guess it is Wolf.

She sits next to him and examines his chest, silently. I guess all of his wounds from Pyron aren't healed yet. She gently applies a mixture to different spots on his bare chest. He studies her as she tends to him.

When she's done, they sit in silence for a few moments watching the flames. Then she strolls out of the cave and onto the beach. Hiding is just an extra precaution because Ameana is too deep in thought to see me.

The wind blows carelessly through her hair as she stands on the soft sand overlooking the waves. Wolf stands up by the fire and walks towards me. I quickly hide in the shadows, not wanting to interfere with the couple.

I was wrong about the guy being Wolf. I was wrong about the guy being an angel. Rage emerges from the cave shirtless and heads toward Ameana by the water.

He embraces her from behind. She leans into him. He nuzzles the slope of her neck slowly. She puts her hand through his hair, silently seeking out his kiss. He hungrily complies. She inhales deeply and closes her eyes.

Ameana is in heaven…with a demon.

I leave them alone and take off into the sky. I could have stopped them but for some reason, I didn't. I'm not sure why. However it plays out, it's gonna have to be dealt with in the light and not on Earth. I pick up speed and head to West Africa.

When I get to the meeting point just outside of Ghana, I find Ameana standing next to Miku, looking flushed. Jay stands proudly with Isabelle. But there is no sign of Rio.

"Have you guys seen him?" I ask.

"We talked a few minutes ago. He was on his way," Miku says.

I call his cell. He picks up on the first ring.

"Where are you? The light is coming. We need to be in it, you know that," I scold him.

"I was helping some kids trying to escape a fire a few miles outside of Moscow. I didn't realize it was that late."

"Did everyone make it out okay?"

"Yeah."

"Were any of them supposed to die?"

"No, Marcus. I wouldn't do that again."

"Okay, we'll wait for you."

"No, you guys go. I'll be right behind you."

"No, I don't want to leave anyone on Earth for any reason. We came together, we leave together."

"Did you say goodbye to Emmy?" he asks hesitantly.

Damn, how can just hearing her name hurt?

"She doesn't want to see me, Rio."

"Do you want to know what her Wave says?"

It would just make it harder to walk away from "us."

"No, I don't. Just get here so we can go, okay?"

"Okay, be there in a sec."

At exactly midnight, a brilliant light streams down into the forest. I tell the group we need to wait for Rio and they all agree. The council will be slightly pissed but given everything we've been through, I think they can cut us some slack.

"Isabelle, you can go ahead of us," Jay says.

"Aw, come with me," she asks sweetly.

All of us make childish sounds and cheer them on. Embarrassed, Jay plays it off like it's nothing, but I can tell he's gonna give her his Rah very soon.

"No, it's cool. We'll catch up," I tell him.

The two take off into the light. Their bodies glow, become small beams of light, and then disappear.

A few minutes later, we see Rio flying towards us. I'm relieved because I was about to give in and go see her, knowing that it would only make things worse. We wait for Rio to land so we can all take off into the light together.

But Rio never lands because at the very moment his foot is about to touch the ground, a nuclear kind of explosion goes off in the sky.

The bomb sends us hurtling into the air without control. We're blown miles away from where we once were. The sky splits wide open and millions of snowflakes fall down on us.

I look closer and realize it's not snow falling from the sky, but angel debris. The explosion caused massive damage to the angels in the surrounding area. We run back to the site to find out what is going on.

The forest looks like an angels' mass grave. Their bodies lie lifeless and in pieces. The first living angel we see is Jay.

His left wing has been blown off. His right arm hangs uselessly at his side. But the worst thing isn't Jay's missing left wing or his broken arm, the worst is the expression on his face. He is in utter disbelief. We surround our bleeding friend and teammate.

"What the hell just happened?" we ask.

Jay doesn't respond immediately. It's like he forgot how to form sentences. Finally he streams some words together and tries to make us understand.

"We went to the light…found the Sisters…They had an orb, big, big, orb…Chance said Godfather told them the time is now…no more hiding in shadows…no more outcast…the age of the Quo has finally come… they got the Amulet and now they are free from their winged oppressors… they said 'the winged ones will no longer be permitted into the light.'"

Jay stops as if the memory is too much to relive. Ameana pushes him to keep going. His voice is frail from shock.

"Chance called the orb to life, it glowed. Then Choice harvested this massive energy of rage, she must have been saving it up for Cycles. And then Charity, she used her ability to boost the power of others, together they…they…"

"What did they do, Jay?" Miku asks, clearly afraid of the answer.

"They made a bomb a trillion times more destructive than the ones made by humans. They set it off and…"

"How many angels are hurt up there?" I ask him.

"You don't understand," Jay says, making eye contact for the first time. "Marcus, they're dead," he says.

"Who's dead?"

"Isabelle. The Originals. The Paras of Daraquin. The council."

"The council?" the twins ask.

"Guys…*everyone* is dead."

Chapter Nineteen: Going Home

We ask Jay again because his answer is simply too difficult to digest. But no matter how many times or how many different ways, the answer is still the same:

"The Quo came in and just blew angels up," he says.

"And they said 'Godfather' told them to do this?" I ask.

"Yes."

"Where is he?" I order.

The team all start speaking at once. It finally begins to sink in: we have lost most of our friends, families, and loved ones, not to mention the council.

"Will Omnis come down?" Miku asks.

"Why? He never has before," Rio says bitterly.

"I don't know what Omnis is going to do, but I damn well know what I'm going to do," I vow.

The rage that builds up in all of us is palpable. Jay, having seen the attack in person, is growing more and more murderous by the minute.

"We need to go to Adam City, find the Sisters, and make them understand the power of angels," Ameana threatens with venom.

Jay tries to recount what he read in the history book regarding the Quo. Unfortunately, he's too distracted to really be of help. The twins are busy calling around to see if they can find out exactly how many angels survived the massacre.

Finally, the twins are able to string together pieces of information from different parts of the world, from angels who managed to escape the attack.

"Eighty percent of the angel population has been murdered," Rio informs us.

Eighty percent???

Armed with the devastating new information, when we get to Adam City, we destroy everything in our path. We call out for the three murderers to appear.

The temple is empty. The three sisters are nowhere to be found.

"Well, where the hell is this Godfather? What kind of malevolent evil exterminates over twenty million angels?" Rio asks, more pissed than I've ever seen him.

"I don't know who the Godfather is, but when I find him, he should run," Jay swears.

"They're not here, we need to head back in the city and search everywhere. We start with the market and we don't stop until we find this evil and cut him down like we did all the other evil that stood in our way!"

The team cheers wildly and starts to march out of the temple. That's when I hear a conversation taking place in one of the back rooms. I direct the team to where I heard the voices.

Behind the door, we hear a man say:

"Yes, I will go get it for you right now, Godfather."

Then we hear a door open and close.

"The Godfather is in there," Jay says.

What kind of evil would kill millions of innocent angels? The Godfather has to be an evil more destructive and deadly than even Kairo. We will take him down. The Godfather must be killed at all costs.

I kick in the door to confront the evil entity.

He sits calmly on a chair and greets me.

"Hello, Marcus."

"Hello, Sage."

END OF BOOK FOUR

OTHER BOOKS BY LOLA STVIL

THE GUARDIANS SERIES

Book 1: The Girl
Book 2: The Fallout
Book 3: The Turn
Book 4: The Triplex
Book 5, Part 1: The Quo
Book 5, Part 2: The Lyris
Book 6, Part 1: The Shoma
Book 6, Part 2: The Nycren

THE NORU SERIES

Book 1: Blue Rose
Book 2: The Last Akon
Book 3: Fall of the Chosen
Book 4: When Angels Break
Book 5: Ways of the Wicked
Book 6: Rise of the Alago

ABOUT THE AUTHOR

Lola StVil is a *New York Times* and *USA Today* bestselling author living in California. She enjoys spending time with her family and staying in touch with her readers.

www.ingramcontent.com/pod-product-compliance
Lightning Source LLC
Chambersburg PA
CBHW072222150726
48002CB00005B/1931